THE DUKE'S DEFIANT ANGEL

Dukes Gone Dirty
Book 1

Bella Moxie

ARE YOU SIGNED UP FOR DRAGONBLADE'S BLOG?

You'll get the latest news and information on exclusive giveaways, exclusive excerpts, coming releases, sales, free books, cover reveals and more.

Check out our complete list of authors, too!

No spam, no junk. That's a promise!

Sign Up Here

www.dragonbladepublishing.com

Dearest Reader;

Thank you for your support of a small press. At Dragonblade Publishing, we strive to bring you the highest quality Historical Romance from some of the best authors in the business. Without your support, there is no 'us', so we sincerely hope you adore these stories and find some new favorite authors along the way.

Happy Reading!

CEO, Dragonblade Publishing

CHAPTER ONE

THERE WERE TWO types of gentlemen in attendance at the Daltons' ball, those looking for a lady to fuck and those hoping to wed.

William Cooper, the Duke of Raffian, had always prided himself on being a member of the former, far more desirable club. His friends, too. But alas, that was no longer the case.

"Are you certain this is wise, Raff?" the Marquess of Hayden slurred beside him. "You can't really mean to wed."

Benedict gave a huff of amusement on his other side.

Raff shot Hayden a sidelong glare. He clearly wasn't taking this new mission seriously if he was already so far in his cups.

"I've made my decision, Hayden," Raff said. "And you're meant to find a wife this Season, as well, if you'll recall." He turned his glare on Benedict, the new Earl of Foster. "We all are. We had an agreement."

Hayden frowned, rocking dangerously far back on his heels and nearly bumping into a society matron, who scowled at all three of them as she passed.

"Pardon me, my lady," Raff said on his friend's behalf.

The older woman's scowl faded fast. "Oh, no need to apologize, Your Grace. We are so grateful you and your friends decided to join us this evening."

"Is that so?" He searched the woman's round face for any hint of recognition. For the life of him, he could not recall this woman, but she seemed well acquainted with him.

"Oh, yes, Your Grace." Her voice was so high and cheerful it bordered on shrill, no doubt to be heard over the clamor of voices around them in this ballroom crush. "My nieces would be delighted to make your acquaintance," she continued, her eyes lighting with a fervor that made his stomach twist with dread.

He took a sip of his drink. Perhaps Hayden had the right of it. Some spirits might help ease this torture.

Word had spread quickly, it seemed, that the three infamous rakes were finally ready to settle. It was a good thing they'd banded together to get through this Season because the marriage-minded mamas were circling like hawks.

So far, he'd had an earl's daughter, a viscount's niece, and a duke's cousin paraded before him—a veritable cornucopia of marriageable young ladies.

And then there was the main course, as it were. The Viscount Dalton's only daughter, who, rumor had it, was a diamond of the first water.

The *ton* had been chattering on about her beauty and grace for weeks now leading up to the start of the Season, and Raff had to admit even he was mildly intrigued to see what all the fuss was about.

"...and then, of course, her sister, my youngest niece," the older woman was saying. "She's a delight to watch on the dance floor. Such grace. Such manners. I'm certain you'll agree."

She looked to Hayden, whose gaze was unfocused as he wobbled precariously in place. Then to Raff, with a simpering smile he did not even try to return. Last, she looked to Benedict, but her gaze darted away quickly—rudely, even—at the sight of his scars.

"We look forward to meeting them," Raff finally said, for the sole purpose of urging her along.

"I don't know how I let you talk me into this," Benedict growled as the matron finally walked away with promises of introductions to her nieces.

This ball marked Benedict's first outing in society since the catastrophic accident which had left him the new earl.

It seemed he hadn't missed it.

Not that Raff could blame him. Events like this evening's ball were tedious enough without the stares and the whispers that followed in Benedict's wake.

"I already told you, Benedict," Raff said. "If one of us must fall, we all go down together."

Benedict's answer was a grunt.

"Awfully sporting of us, I'd say," Hayden said, a drunken grin spreading lazily across features that the more dimwitted ladies of the *ton* referred to as angelic.

If that angel in question were Satan, then perhaps Raff would agree.

Hayden's taste for debauchery only rivaled Raff's. But, all the ladies of society saw was that the Marquess of Hayden was unusually handsome with his thick brown hair and sharp, regal features. Charming, too.

Benedict, on the other hand…

"I didn't ask you to do this," Benedict reminded them as he eyed the growing crowd warily, his low voice curt. "Either of you."

Raff ignored this. Benedict had always been a bit of a brute, but before the accident that had left him scarred as well as titled, he hadn't been nearly as churlish.

A wife would help, no doubt. The poor bloke needed someone to help run his household. Preferably someone who was not his mother and who did not blame him for the loss of his father and brother.

A young lady with bright red hair and a hideous smile batted her eyelashes at Hayden as she passed, then promptly buried her head behind a fan to giggle with her friend.

"I shall never survive this Season," Hayden said with a sigh.

"This is our first ball," Raff said. "Don't tell me you're already waving the white flag."

Hayden scoffed. "Just don't see why the hurry, that's all."

Raff's jaw clenched. The hurry, as Hayden put it, was for Benedict's sake, a point he'd prefer not to callously point out in front of the earl.

Besides, if Hayden weren't so soused, he'd remember why they'd agreed to this and why now.

"Are you sure we couldn't put this off for one more Season?" This time, Hayden tipped sideways as he spoke. He might have ended up on the floor if Benedict hadn't caught him by a shoulder and set him upright.

"Not one of us is getting any younger," Raff said. "We've already put this off as long as we can."

"Yes, yes," Hayden said with a wave of his hand that would have smacked Raff in the nose if he hadn't moved out of the way. "I know we're not young lads anymore, however—"

"Benedict needs a wife, and we all know it," Raff said, losing the battle with tact. His friends knew him well enough to know it had been a losing battle to begin with. He was not known for his diplomacy. And why should he be? He'd inherited the dukedom at a young age and had become accustomed to having his way with a single command.

Having to explain himself and his decisions, even to his friends, was not a part of his nature. It was as vile a thought as asking for permission or begging for forgiveness.

He was, as Benedict liked to point out, a stubborn and high-handed arse.

Not that Benedict was much better. Perhaps not high-handed, but the man was terse, at best. And that was how a friend might describe him. His short temper and curt manners might not have counted against him when he still had his dark, brooding good looks. But now…

Well, the title would have to suffice. Benedict certainly wouldn't be winning a bride with his looks anymore, and definitely not with his boorish manners. Still, there were plenty of ladies who'd overlook all that to be a countess.

Raff's gaze swept over the crowd for just such a lady. A kind one, preferably. One with an abundance of patience and good humor. Someone sweet and gentle who could provide some comfort in that drafty, morbid old estate in the country where Benedict had been spending all his time.

No such woman magically materialized before him. More the pity. He took another swig of his drink. He wasn't enjoying this outing any more than his friends.

Hayden was still wearing a sullen frown, and Raff patted his shoulder in commiseration. "Sorry to say it, but you need a wife, too, old chum."

"And you, Raff?" Benedict asked. "Isn't it high time you wed, as well?" For the first time all night, there was a hint of amusement in that low growl of a voice, and that had Raff smiling slightly.

It was mocking amusement, a jest at his expense. But Raff was relieved to hear it, all the same.

"And me," Raff agreed. "I have but one true duty to the dukedom, and I well know it."

And alas, to sire an heir required taking a wife.

If there'd been some way around that, Raff would have been the first to find it.

"What about Malcolm?" Hayden asked, his lower lip sticking out like a petulant child. "Why doesn't he have to join us in this marriage business?"

The Earl of Fallenmore's heir was typically the fourth member of their pack, and his absence tonight could be felt.

Benedict's brows came down as he turned to Hayden. "Because Malcolm's already engaged, remember?"

"Oh yes. I'd forgotten. That viscount's daughter from the neighboring property." Hayden's gaze grew distant. "That must be nice. Having a pretty young thing all picked out and waiting for you."

Raff gave a huff of amusement. "You'd rather your parents

had arranged a match for you when you were still in the nursery, eh?"

Hayden ignored that. "Bloody good luck on his part," he muttered. "I'd bet Malcolm's down at Vestry Lane even now, laughing at us."

Benedict gave a grunt in return.

Vestry Lane was a stretch of London that held a world of sin along its seedy cobblestone streets and back alleys. What had started out as a few blocks filled with gaming hells, brothels, and pubs had become a haven for gentlemen of all classes and stations, seeking to satisfy their vices.

Ladies, too, he supposed. Though most who visited Vestry Lane could hardly be called ladies in any true sense of the word.

That was likely where Malcolm was off to this evening, and it was where they all wished they could be. Where they *would* be if Raff hadn't insisted that this was the Season he finally did right by his title and produced an heir.

It was time, though, for all of them.

"You'll thank me," Raff said with the unwavering confidence for which he was known. "Once you have your heir and your spare, and you go back to tupping that widow of yours with a clear conscience."

"I s'pose you're right that we're not getting any younger," Hayden agreed with a resigned sigh.

"Quite so," Raff said. Truthfully, this had been a long time coming. There was little expected of any of them anymore—years of being rakish, irredeemable cads had ensured that. For Hayden and Raff, particularly, they'd ensured the real work of running their estates was being well handled by solicitors and estate managers and the like. They were little more than figureheads these days. But sadly, siring a legitimate heir wasn't a task they could delegate.

As the eldest of them all, the clock had been ticking on Raff's bachelorhood for years now. The need to sire an heir had been hanging over him like an executioner's ax, and there was no putting it off any longer.

But his life would not end with a wife, he reminded himself, even as his gut coiled with dread.

Just as soon as this business was dealt with, he could get back to the gaming hells and brothels on Vestry Lane, while his wife's belly swelled with his babe.

He took another swig of his drink. The sooner they got this marriage business sorted, the better for everyone.

"That Everton chit won't stop staring at me," Hayden complained.

"She's staring at *me*," Benedict said.

No doubt he was right. Raff had caught any number of ladies and gentlemen stealing glances at the scandal-ridden new earl. But this rabid curiosity on the *ton*'s behalf was at least partially Benedict's fault. Raff had been trying to get him out of his country estate and back into society for months now. The longer he'd hidden away, the more curious the *ton* had become about the formerly dashing rake who was now covered in scars and burns from the fire.

Raff shifted so the Evertons and their daughter were staring at his back. "This doesn't need to be torture," he said. "We just need to get it done. And at least none of us is in need of a substantial dowry, we've no lack of good connections to make up for…" He threw back the last of his drink in one fortifying gulp. "No father with a bit of sense would deny us."

Hayden murmured something indecipherable in agreement, and even Benedict gave another grunt of acknowledgment.

"So, in short—" Raff cast his arms out wide. "These ladies are ours for the taking. All you have to do is choose the one you wouldn't mind bedding more than once, and we'll be done with this whole sordid affair."

A stir on the far side of the ballroom had them glancing over. The crowd shifted, gathering around the bottom of the curved staircase.

Everyone was waiting to catch a glimpse of *her*. Miss Evangeline Dalton. The talk of the town.

Raff set a hand on Hayden's shoulder when he went lopsided again. "Steady, old chap. There will be plenty of time for real fun later, once we've done our duty for the night and—"

His words died in his mouth as a young lady made her descent on the staircase at the far end of the room.

Hayden was saying something about what he planned to do when they escaped this place. Benedict muttered something about how he couldn't dance with a woman if she was too terrified to look at him.

But Raff was barely listening to either.

His gaze was ensnared as a slim figure in a pale gold gown descended the stairs. Her hair was as pale as moonlight, her skin creamy. Her cheeks and lips were tinged with pink, and even from where he stood, he could see the perfection of her face. From a lush cupid's bow of a mouth to the delicately arched brows...she was perfection.

A living, breathing work of art.

And that was just her face. He let his gaze move over the rest of her hungrily, drinking her in from the magnificent curve of her breasts, to the long, slender neck, and down to the tiny waist, where her gown nipped in before cascading out and over her hips.

What he would not give to see the curves of her bottom half.

Indeed, his mouth had gone dry from wanting. He wanted to see all of her. Those succulent curves spilling over in his hands, the downy curls that covered the heart of her femininity, the soft curve of her thighs as they spread for him.

All of it. All of her.

He wanted it all.

"I told you she was pretty," an elderly gentleman said to his friend.

Heat clawed through Raff's veins, spreading to his limbs and making his cock so hard it had his jaw clenching in pain.

Pretty, they'd said? What a tepid word. She wasn't merely

pretty. She was dazzling in her beauty.

She was incomparable. And he'd never wanted anything more.

Raff's lips curved up in a smirk.

As simple as that. He'd been so dreading the ordeal of seeking out a bride, and he'd found her just like that.

This was the one.

He almost pitied the other ladies here tonight, for this delightful creature had just won the role of duchess without so much as trying.

"You all right, Raff?" Hayden said. "You look like you've seen a ghost."

Raff shook his head. He couldn't tear his eyes from her as she reached the bottom of the curved staircase, her eyes cast down demurely, her lips set in a sweet, obedient smile.

"Not a ghost," he murmured to his friends. "An angel."

They laughed—no doubt they thought he was in jest. But even if her sweet nature were not so very clear to see, even at a distance, he already knew for a fact that she'd granted him mercy. Truly, this gorgeous little creature had just saved him from what had threatened to be a torturous Season of dancing and small talk and courting.

Now he could skip all of that because his choice was clear.

He'd found his duchess.

The lady in question gazed out at the gathered crowd with wide eyes and pink lips that curved ever so slightly at the corners in a shy smile that tugged at his chest. That sweet, hesitant smile made him want to gather her into his arms and assure her that all would be well.

The swell of her breasts, which he had a far better view of now that she'd turned to face the crowd—that also made him want to gather her into his arms, so he could feel those soft curves pressed against him.

That body was his. Only his. Only he would ever touch it.

A wave of possessiveness swept over him so abruptly, it stole his breath and tightened his every muscle.

Bloody hell. His hands were balled into fists, ready to fight any man who thought to take her from him.

She was *his*. And he ached to claim her right here and right now.

All at once, his mind was filled with the vision of taking her hard right where she stood on the stairway. He'd hitch up those skirts, spread those thighs, and thrust himself into her, so everyone knew she was his.

He let out a shaky exhale as he battled for control.

The thought was madness, and he knew it. This wasn't ancient times. He couldn't just lay claim to a woman and drag her bag to his home.

He straightened his cravat as he kept his gaze fixed on his prize.

Despite the rumors of his rakish ways, he was still a duke. He knew how to be civilized when the occasion called for it. He'd do this the right way.

A searing heat gripped his loins as her lips spread into a wider smile at something her mother said.

Quickly, he amended. He'd do this the right way, but he'd do it quickly. The sooner he had her in his bed, the better.

"She is a beauty, I'll grant you that," Hayden said.

"She's perfect," Raff said, his voice gruffer and more harsh than intended.

He was dimly aware of his friends exchanging looks behind his back.

But she *was* his.

His choice had been made.

He didn't rush to her side, though. He let the other gentlemen crowd ahead as he reveled in the sight of her from afar.

Unlike Hayden, she truly was the image of an angel with her white-gold locks. He could see the bright blue sparkle of her eyes and make out the high cheekbones and pointed chin. This close, he could see that her lips were a luscious red.

She was the picture of decorum and innocence in her pale gown, but her lips...

Her lips made his imagination run wild. Full and pouty, as though she'd been kissed hard and left wanting more. With a shock of heat, he saw it clearly. Those swollen lips parting for his thick shaft. Those pretty eyes widening with innocence, her cheeks turning pink with desire as she took him into her hot, welcoming mouth.

Oh yes, her pretty little mouth was made for him and him alone.

"She's mine," he said, lest his friends were forming ideas of their own.

"You've already chosen?" Hayden laughed. "But the Season has only just begun."

"Doesn't matter," Raff said, his gaze seemingly unable to be torn away from the delicate little maiden.

She was a rare gem. Precious. Desired. The best that London society had to offer.

"I'm going to claim her tonight," he said.

"Be reasonable, chum," Benedict said. "Marriage is a business arrangement. There'll be negotiations and contracts to deal with. Don't give her father a reason—"

"It's done," he said, waving a hand to brush aside his friend's words. Benedict meant well. He was merely trying to keep Raff from giving away his upper hand or making a hasty decision before he'd seen all his cards.

But that was the difference between Raff and his friends.

He was decisive. A man of action. He knew what he wanted, and he got it.

He took it.

Raff strode toward the young lady now, ignoring everyone who tried to stop him to talk and those awaiting an introduction to his lady. He was a man with a singular purpose, and he was not one to be swayed once his mind was made up.

Whether it was a mistress, a whore, an antique, or a hunting dog—he always took what he wanted.

And he'd never wanted anything more than he wanted Miss Evangeline Dalton.

CHAPTER TWO

THE STARES WERE too much.

Evangeline's hands trembled as her father grasped her elbow to lead her further into the ballroom.

"It's one night, Angie," her father murmured so only she could hear.

"Yes, Father." Her chin came up even as her skin crawled under the weight of their stares. The muscles in her legs twitched, ready to run. Her lungs hitched as she tried to draw in a deep breath—difficult to do with her stays cinched so tight.

Her father was right. It was one night. Only one night.

She could withstand anything for one night. Couldn't she?

Her breath left her in a whoosh of air as her gaze collided with one stare in particular.

She looked away quickly. The man was staring so intently, he was bordering on rude. But the tall, formidable-looking fellow wasn't among the crowd currently jostling for her attention, and so she forced herself not to look again.

Even when she was smiling demurely at the gentlemen around her, half-listening to her father's introductions to the men he considered friends, she was keenly aware of the man with the golden eyes.

That's how they'd looked in the flickering candlelight from the chandelier, at least.

Like a predator's eyes, they'd been fixed on her as if he could see straight through her forced smile to the truth that lay beneath.

She was miserable.

She was terrified.

She wished more than anything that she could have avoided this entire affair. But of course, they had to put on the pretense, at least, that she was an eligible young lady looking for a match.

Even her parents weren't yet aware that she'd already found her husband.

She curtsied before a baron who told her he and her father had been friends since their school days. He went on to tell her a story from their youth...while eyeing her decolletage with a predatory gleam of his own.

A glance around her revealed more hungry stares.

Predators, the lot of them.

Her knees trembled as the foolish thought took hold. For one moment, she imagined they were closing in on her.

Don't be daft.

This was not a hunt, and she was not some fox on the run.

She had nothing to fear. It was just her shy nature, that was all. Painfully shy, according to her mother. Always had been. And no amount of lessons in etiquette and elocution had driven it out of her.

So, no. It wasn't just the men she feared. It was all of them. Lords and ladies alike. Every time she risked a glance around her, she caught ladies staring with just as much unabashed curiosity, though perhaps a little less leering.

Your own fault, her mother had informed her before she'd come down the stairs for her grand entrance. *If you'd socialized more with the ladies of the* ton *like other girls your age, this Season wouldn't be such a hardship for you.*

Perhaps so. But Evangeline had always preferred their country manor to the townhome in London. And she'd preferred the company there, as well.

Once again, she risked a glance around her, hoping to see the man who would be her husband. Albert had promised he'd come. As the second son of a baron, he might not have been as high-ranking as her father's friends, but her parents had never been so worried about titles.

Besides, surely what mattered most was Albert's kindness to her. His affection for her was indisputable. And one she proved that meeting other gentlemen would not sway her, as her parents believed, surely her father would relent and agree to their marrying.

She just had to make it through this one night, that was all.

She merely had to hold up her end of this bargain.

And she would. She lifted her chin. She'd do it for Albert.

For him, she could summon her courage. It would be easier to withstand the attention if he were here, though. His support, even if from a distance, would be most heartening.

"...you truly have grown into quite the beauty," an elderly gentleman was saying.

He held her hand in his, and his grip was crushing.

"Thank you, my lord," she murmured.

When his next words were directed at her father, she turned her gaze once more to the crowd. But in her search for Albert, she caught *his* gaze again.

She did not know who he was, but she did not like him. She didn't have to know him to know that the way he looked at her was outright devilish. His smirk spoke of conceit, and the tilt of his chin as he looked down his nose told anyone in the nearby vicinity that he was of importance.

She sniffed as she looked away. He might have been handsome enough, she supposed, if one liked older men.

Granted, he was not as ancient as the viscount before her, who had yet to let go of her gloved hand. But he had creases near his eyes, and his dark hair had a sprinkle of gray at the temples.

Too old for her liking. And even if she found him attractive, she would never be tempted to go near a man like him. His features were hard. The set of his jaw unforgiving.

This was not a predator who'd merely capture his prey.

He'd break it. Devour it.

She shivered as she tore her gaze away, her throat working as she tried to swallow.

"And of course, you remember Lady Stanza," her mother said from her right.

"Of course," she murmured as she curtsied.

Truly, she was behaving like a child. She was flanked by her parents and surrounded by high-standing members of society who merely wished to know her.

And at any moment, she'd glance up to see Albert coming toward her to claim a dance. Her parents might not have wished for her to rush into an engagement without a proper Season, but soon enough, they'd come to understand that she wasn't about to be swayed by any other man. No matter the title, no matter the wealth.

And then…well, then they would not reject his suit.

Not so long as she'd done her part.

It seemed an eternity had passed before the crowd around her eased, and music began to play at the far end of the ballroom.

For the first time since she'd arrived, she could breathe. And for the first time in far too long, she was alone.

Well, surrounded by a crush of guests, but at least she did not have her father's hand at her back, nudging her toward an endless stream of people. Even her mother had wandered off to a nearby cluster of matrons. Evangeline could hear her talking animatedly about all the preparations involved for tonight's ball.

For one blessed moment, Evangeline could breathe.

"You have outshone the stars tonight, Miss Dalton." The low voice beside her made her start.

Eyes wide with surprise, she turned to face…*him.*

The man with the fierce stare who'd been frightening her from afar from the moment she'd entered the room.

She met his dark gaze and then looked around frantically for her parents. Surely the gentleman would wish to be introduced properly, and—

"Allow me to introduce myself, since your family seems preoccupied," he said.

Her lips parted in shock.

He meant to…introduce himself?

Her heart raced at his audacity.

Before she could recover, he had her hand in his and was leaning over it. "William Cooper, the Duke of Raffian."

She blinked once. Twice. The Duke of…

The blood rushed from her head so quickly, she nearly lost her balance.

"Ah, I see you've heard of me." His gaze met hers with wicked humor.

She couldn't respond. All she managed was a nod. Had she heard of him? Of course, she had. She knew his name well, along with a few others who were oft mentioned alongside him.

Namely, Lucifer, Beelzebub, and Mephistopheles.

He lifted her hand and glanced meaningfully toward the dance floor where the first strains of a waltz were underway. "May I?"

The terror that had been plaguing her all day was so quickly replaced by fury, she felt all that lost blood rush back into her face. Into her cheeks, more specifically, and the knave before her chuckled in response.

"Have I scandalized you, my dear girl?" he asked.

She swallowed hard. *Yes.* He had. The man hadn't even waited for a proper introduction. And there was no way she could refuse him a dance, as he had to know.

He was a duke.

He was *the* duke, according to her mother and her friends. Powerful and wealthy beyond belief. She cast a quick glance at her mother, who was watching her, her brows arched in eager anticipation.

Scandalous as his approach might be, his seeking her out was an honor.

At least, in her mother's eyes.

There was only one acceptable answer.

Evangeline forced a tremulous smile. "It would be my pleasure, Your Grace."

He chuckled again as he drew her close. Too close.

Anger pulsed in her veins just as surely as terror. Who did this man think he was? He was thwarting all the rules. Even as she thought it, he slid an arm about her waist. To anyone else, it might have seemed he was guiding her toward the dance floor, but she felt the heat of his hand sliding over her waist like a brand.

He held her so close, she could feel the solid heat of his chest against her side, and the scent of unfamiliar male invaded her senses. It was some mix of cologne, liquor, and leather, and it made her feel even more like she was being engulfed in the man's grip.

The crowd parted for them, and the stares—she turned her face away instinctively, but that seemed to make him think she enjoyed his hold on her because he made a sound of approval as he tugged her even closer. "I have you, Angel. You've nothing to fear."

She lifted her head then and found herself gaping at him as he took her hand in his and placed the other on her low back, ready to lead her in a waltz.

You've nothing to fear.

Was he in jest? Everyone had heard the rumors about the immoral duke and his libertine friends. According to the scandal sheets, he was rarely sober, never at home, and always connected to some tawdry tale involving opera singers and the like.

He smiled down at her just as the music swelled, and they moved as one into the dance. His smile was no doubt meant to be reassuring, but it had her heart fluttering like a hummingbird trying to be free.

She looked away quickly from that all-seeing gaze and the all-knowing smile. So very knowing. His smug demeanor proved to be her salvation, cutting through her fear and sparking indignation. Her spine stiffened with pride, and while she couldn't quite meet his gaze, she held her chin high all the same.

"Such a darling young lady," he said, his voice a murmur, and she couldn't tell if he was talking to her or herself. "Your parents should not have left you alone like that."

She peeked up at him and looked away as if scalded. She *had* been scalded. That look in his eyes, the unbridled heat. Her cheeks burned from it, and her breathing grew more shallow by the second.

Oh, where was Albert? She glanced around as subtly as she could, but all she saw were more stares.

Meanwhile, the duke asked her questions about herself that she dutifully answered with as few words as possible. *Yes, Your Grace. No, Your Grace. As you say, Your Grace.* Mere whispers as she prayed for this torture to end.

Couldn't he feel the stares? Didn't he mind the whispers?

No. She suspected not.

"Do you not enjoy all this attention, Miss Dalton?" he asked as he swept her across the floor.

She dipped her head, ready to say, *No, Your Grace* once more. But she was taken aback when his dancing swept her right off the dance floor, so they were standing next to the glass doors leading to the veranda.

"Allow me to steal you away then," he said.

She stared up at him in horror. Had he truly just said that? She wasn't certain now whether it was terror or anger that made her tremble. Perhaps it was a touch of both.

Surely this man was mad. What kind of lunatic threatened to steal a young lady away? Even if he were in jest, he'd gone too far.

He reached out and touched her cheek, the back of his gloved hand tracing over her skin and down her jaw as if it were his right.

She forgot how to breathe.

Her heart slammed against her ribcage, and heat flooded her neck and cheeks.

The audacity of this man!

His smile hitched up on one side in a crooked grin that seemed to say he knew precisely what she was thinking. He knew she was terrified, and that amused him.

Oh, where was Albert?

Her mind went blank for a moment as his thumb brushed her lower lip. His touch was gentle but so inappropriate, she knew not how to respond.

And then again… *Where is Albert?*

She took a step away as she prayed that wherever he was, he had not seen that intimate, possessive display. He'd understand it wasn't her fault. Of course he would. Dear Albert was nothing if not understanding. He'd even taken her parents' decision to hold off on accepting his proposal until after this Season in stride.

But all the same, she'd never give him reason to doubt her fidelity or her love.

She took another step back, her promises to Albert giving her renewed courage.

"Come outside with me, Miss Dalton," the duke said.

It was not a request.

"Your Grace, I cannot," she said with as much pride as she could muster.

His low laughter was tolerant but patronizing. The kind of laugh one would use when a child insisted there were ghosts in the attic. "Sweet Evangeline."

She gasped at his use of her name. But truly, did she expect anything less than the most outrageous manners from the rogue after all he'd done thus far?

"Surely your father would not argue if you wished to steal a moment alone with the duke who has singled you out?"

Evangeline's eyes widened. Now she knew for certain she was trapped in a nightmare. Or some terrible melodrama. "I ought to get back to my parents before they miss me," she said.

He smiled, a huff of laughter making her wonder if he were mocking her. "Very well. You can tell your mother you have impressed me with your dutiful manners."

She took another step away from him, ready to run and fighting a horrible surge of hysterical laughter at his hubris. She hadn't the faintest desire to impress him and even less desire to be singled out by him.

She dipped her head politely, though, ready to flee.

"And you can tell your father that he need not worry about your virtue, dear one. I've already planned to speak with him."

Evangeline's chest rose and fell quickly as his words settled over her.

Speak to her father? Surely he couldn't mean…

He did not intend to court her. Did he?

The arrogant old beast had the nerve to wink at her before giving her a short gallant bow. "I'll be seeing you again soon, my dear."

His words echoed in his wake like a vow.

Like a threat.

She gave her head a shake before hurrying back to her parents. There was no way she'd marry a man like that. And no one would ever make her.

CHAPTER THREE

H AYDEN PEERED AT Raff through the thick cloud of smoke that hung in the air around their table at the club. His brows knitted in confusion. "What do you mean, *she said no?*"

Raff took a puff from his cigar before holding it before him to study it. A loud roar came from the room next door where some dancers were putting on a show for the clientele. This gaming hell on Vestry Lane was as far from Mayfair as a man could get, and yet he still could not escape thoughts of Miss Evangeline Dalton.

He couldn't escape talking about her either, it seemed.

"Exactly what I said," Raff said. He tried to keep his voice even, but he couldn't hide his frustration.

Two weeks since he'd chosen his bride. The banns ought to have been posted by now, the contract signed, and the deal as good as done.

Malcolm frowned in incomprehension as he threw some coin down on the table for the next wager. "But that makes no sense."

"I know," Raff said.

Hayden squinted at him. "But you're a duke."

"I *know*," Raff said again.

All three of them sat in silence as they tried to make sense of it. A viscount's daughter, pretty as she might be, did not say no to a duke.

"Did you speak to her yourself?" Malcolm asked. His own fiancée was waiting at their neighboring estate like a good little girl, while Raff's intended bride was…

Well, he had no idea what she was up to. He hadn't seen her since the night of the Daltons' ball, and he'd made a point of going to every boring society event he was invited to over the last fortnight. And at every soiree and dinner party, he had perfectly lovely young ladies thrust in front of him, all too eager to catch his fancy.

But the one he wanted…

He stubbed his cigar out with a growl.

The one wanted had not attended. Not a single outing. He was starting to wonder if he'd imagined the angel in his arms.

"I'll take that as a no," Malcolm said. "You have not spoken to her, have you?" He sank back in his seat with a smirk. With his black hair and dark eyes, the Earl of Fallenmore's only son and heir looked like the very devil himself there in the smoky room.

"She said no to the Duke of Raffian," Hayden said with a shake of his head. "I cannot believe it."

Raff's friends shared a look before bursting out into a laugh.

At his expense.

Raff ignored them. "Where's Benedict?"

"Didn't you hear?" Hayden said. "He's left for his country estate. Gave up on all this marriage mart business while you were busy chasing after that pretty chit of yours."

"I haven't been—" He cut himself off. Bloody hell. He *had* been chasing after her like some sort of lovestruck fool.

"Hard to believe her parents let her have her way," Malcolm said. "What could they be thinking? It's not as though they could receive a better offer."

"This coming from a man who's been in an arrangement since birth," Raff said. "Of course, you don't understand it."

Raff tapped his cards against the table's edge, ignoring a fight that broke out next to him. Fighting was hardly a rare occurrence here on Vestry Lane. It occurred far more often here than, say,

White's. But what this place lacked in decorum, it more than made up for with other benefits. Like the freedom to say or do anything you wanted without all of society talking about it the next day.

Secrets stayed safe here, thanks to the man who ran it all from behind the scenes. King, they called him. And he might as well have worn a crown for all the fear and respect he garnered from those who worked and lived along this stretch of no-man's land between the slums and the upper crust of society.

No one knew his real name, just as no one knew the name of his head enforcer. That brute was known only as the Beast, and even that moniker was only ever whispered in fear. London's very own terrifying bedtime story.

Malcolm and Hayden were watching him closely. "Don't tell me you're going to let her go without a fight," Malcolm said. "You're not one to give up so easily."

Raff glared at his old friend.

"So? How are you going to convince the girl to give you a chance?" Hayden was clearly enjoying this far more than he ought.

"It's not the girl I need to convince," Raff said, his voice tight with frustration.

Malcolm and Hayden stared at him.

He put down his cards with a sigh. "No young lady in her right mind would say no to a duke."

The other two nodded at this. Every lady wanted to be a duchess. Especially young beauties who'd been raised for it. And Evangeline most certainly had been.

Even now, despite his frustration at being forced to wait for what was his, Raff still felt a smile tugging at his lips at her sweet, demure manners.

He truly had been angry at her parents for letting her out of their sight for even a second. Didn't they know just how fragile a sheltered little beauty like her could be?

She ought to be protected and coddled. And as her father was clearly not doing right by her, it was that much better that he'd decided to make her his.

And she *would* be his. She was exactly what he needed in a wife. Biddable. Beautiful. Obedient. Dutiful.

And beddable in the extreme.

He shifted, adjusting his erection at the mere memory of her. Christ, he needed her in his bed, and he needed it now.

But he suspected her father already knew that.

"I'll bet you everything on this table that it wasn't Miss Dalton saying no," he said.

Hayden stared at him in clear confusion. "Then who was it saying no?"

A muscle in his jaw twitched. "Her father."

"Why wouldn't her father want the likes of you for a son?" Malcolm asked. He sounded so offended on Raff's behalf, Raff was a little touched.

"You've got more money than God," Hayden said.

"Nearly as much power, too," Malcolm added.

"Much as it pains me to admit it, I think Benedict had the right of it." He scowled down at his drink. "I showed too much interest too soon. Now her father no doubt wants to negotiate on the marriage contract."

He sneered as he said it. Truth be told, he couldn't care less about the details of the contract. His friends were not exaggerating about his fortune. He had more money than he knew what to do with. He didn't need her dowry or any of the other inheritance that might come her way.

But her father's rejection roused his suspicions. Only a fool or a desperate man would play games with the Duke of Raffian. The viscount didn't strike him as a fool. So Raff had been doing his digging, and he'd hired King's own man to confirm his suspicions.

"Ah, there he is now," Raff said, straightening as a man strode toward them in this den of vices.

With his hat pulled down low, even with his tall, thin frame, he blended into the shadows. In this world of secrets and coded language, he was known as Tracker. All Raff really knew about him was that he was a former Bow Street Runner before he'd gone to work for King—and any of King's clientele who had need of his skills.

"Your Grace," the man said in a gruff voice as he reached their table.

"Have a seat." Raff gestured to the chair that ought to have been occupied by Benedict—that coward. "Was I right?"

"Yes, Your Grace," Tracker said, his razor-sharp features giving nothing away as he slid a folder in Raff's direction.

"Right about what?" Hayden asked.

But Raff was too busy looking over all Tracker had compiled. What he found made Raff's gut twist with disgust and his blood run hot with anger on his angel's behalf. "Just as I thought," he said. "He's using that sweet little girl of his for his own gain."

"Aren't all fathers?" Malcolm muttered. The bitterness in his voice had Raff and Hayden looking at him sharply. It was no secret that Malcolm's father was a cruel old beast. During their school days, Malcolm had taken pains to avoid his family home. But he was a grown man now, and he waved away their concern. "What is it? What does it say?"

"He's lost nearly everything, the old fool," Raff said, tossing the file down. "He's even used up the money that ought to have gone toward her dowry."

"And he didn't want to tell you," Hayden said, filling in the pieces.

"No doubt he's got one of his old crony friends lined up to take her off his hands, so he doesn't have to admit to what he's done," Malcolm said.

Raff grunted in agreement, but he was still busy staring at the documents compiled before him. He'd no idea how Tracker had gotten his hands on all this, and he didn't rightly care. But now that his suspicions had been confirmed, he'd need to act in haste.

He knew the night of their ball that the Daltons weren't doing a good enough job of protecting his angel. What Tracker found only confirmed it. Shoving away from the table, he nodded at Tracker. "Have King add your pay to my credit."

He dipped his head. "Yes, Your Grace."

His friends were already on their feet. "Where are we going?" Hayden asked.

"Not you, just me," Raff said. "This is a meeting I ought to have alone." A plan took shape and gave him renewed energy. Two weeks had felt like a lifetime, but just as soon as he had her father's signature on the marriage contracts, he'd get himself a special license.

"Place your bets, gents," he said to his friends as he gathered his overcoat and hat. "In less than a fortnight, I'll have that girl in my home and in my bed."

Just the thought had him aching again. He clenched his jaw tight as he donned his hat.

"I'll take that bet," Hayden said as Raff headed toward the door.

"New wager," Malcolm called out in a bored drawl. "How long until she has him on a leash and begging for his freedom?"

"Fuck off," Raff called back to them, but his friends were too busy laughing to hear him.

CHAPTER FOUR

EVANGELINE RESTED HER head against the window's edge as she gazed out at the familiar scene below. The hedges were the same as they'd always been. The garden, too.

She was the only thing that was different.

This could not be her life. She shook her head as tears welled in her eyes. How was this her life?

"Now, now," her mother tutted behind her, kindness gentling her voice. "That's enough of the tears, my dear. Your father made his decision."

And there was no turning back now.

Her mother didn't say it, but she didn't have to. Evangeline's father—her kind, wise, loving father—had forsaken her.

And no one would tell her why.

"No one forces ladies into unwanted matches anymore, Mother," she said. "What Father is doing is barbaric."

Her mother did not disagree, but her silence was telling. While unpleasant, it was hardly unheard of for a father to enforce a marriage contract.

Evangeline had just never expected it from *her* father.

She'd known her entire life that she was not what her parents had wished for in a child. Namely because she was not male— that was the first mark against her. And then she'd not had the demeanor they'd desired. Much as she'd tried, she'd never been able to overcome her shyness.

But even knowing she was not the daughter they'd wished, she'd never been ill-treated. Never been forced to do anything she did not wish. Not until that ill-fated ball.

Not until today's dreaded wedding.

"Please, Mother," she said. "You must see that this is a mistake."

Her mother ignored her as she fussed with the hair accessories on Evangeline's vanity.

Why she continued to argue, she couldn't say. It was futile. A little over a week ago, her father had called her into his office saying he'd had a caller.

She'd barely been able to sit still she'd been so happy.

Of course he'd had a caller. Albert had promised he'd speak to her father again after she'd done her duty by attending the ball in her honor, and he had. "Mr. Foley came to see you," she'd said.

Her father's head had come down with a gruff murmur of assent. "I'm afraid Mr. Foley and I did not see eye to eye when it came to your future happiness, Angie."

She'd felt the floor give way beneath her with her father's words.

He'd denied Albert. Again. For good.

Even now, she still could not understand. Albert was not wealthy, nor was he titled. But he came from a good family, and since he and his family had taken up residence on the neighboring estate a few years back, he'd been a friend to her family.

A friend to *her*.

It was a quiet sort of friendship. And while he'd never done more than steal a kiss of her hand beneath her favorite oak tree, she'd believed it to be as good as done.

He cared for her, and she for him. And…

And she'd been wrong.

In that moment, in her father's study, she'd understood that with alarming clarity. Much as she'd protested and wept and railed throughout the remainder of the conversation, she'd known that her father would not be swayed.

She just hadn't known why.

For *whom*.

But then her father had spoken again, his tone so cold and formal. "The Duke of Raffian has asked for your hand in marriage—"

"Father, no!" This was a mistake. Surely there was some misunderstanding. "We've discussed this. After the ball, when he expressed his interest, I told you clearly that I do not wish to marry that man."

Her father's face had hardened. Gone was the kind, wise, gentle man who'd raised her. In his place was a stranger. "Evangeline, you are little more than a child. You know not what you want."

"I am old enough to marry," she'd argued. "Which means I am old enough to have some say in who I marry."

"You would make a decision based on some childish infatuation?" Her father had openly scoffed, and her already bruised heart had broken. Her stomach had pitched and roiled as he'd continued, telling her how Foley couldn't offer her the life of a duchess. How if Foley truly cared for her, he'd see that—and he had.

Supposedly. According to her father, Foley had relented with grace.

"I don't believe you," she'd said then.

She whispered it again now as she glanced down at the courtyard below.

Guests would already be arriving at the church in Hanover Square. The duke was likely already there, preparing for their nuptials.

"The carriage is waiting," her mother said.

Evangeline sniffed. This was farewell to her family home. After the wedding, she'd be off to the duke's country home for a fortnight. Now her home.

She pressed her lips together to hold back a sob. This was also farewell to the life she'd always known.

Farewell to the life she'd always wanted.

And why? All because some conceited, overbearing duke had decided that he wanted her. He'd claimed her as she might have a doll from a shelf as a child. *Mine*, she'd have said, and then snatched it off the shelf.

That was precisely what the duke had done. And in doing so, he'd ruined her life.

"I hate him," she said in a watery voice.

Her mother's sigh was loud and exasperated. "Dearest, you cannot sulk your way through a wedding to a duke."

Evangeline set her lips in a stubborn line. Her mother had been alternating between understanding and irritated ever since her father's decree.

Mostly, though, her mother was just thrilled at being able to tell her friends that her daughter was to be a duchess.

"No one ever said I had to be happy about being married off to a cruel tyrant with ill manners either," she said.

She sounded like a child, and she knew it. But this was her last chance to speak freely. Her last opportunity, even if futile, to make arguments against this marriage.

Her mother sighed again. "You don't even know the man—"

"Precisely." She whipped around to face her mother. "But from what little I do know, he has the manners of a brute and no consideration at all for my feelings."

Her mother's lips firmed into a thin line. She could not argue that. "Dear, you must not judge the man based solely on gossip and scandal sheets," her mother started.

"I'm not," she said. "I'm judging him based on the way he spoke to me at the ball."

"He took a fancy to you," her mother said. "Any young lady would be delighted to know they'd caught the eye of a duke."

"Well, then let her have him," Evangeline said. Her voice broke with emotion, and she quickly covered her mouth with her hand. "Oh, Mother, I am sorry. I know I'm behaving badly. I just…" She shook her head. "I do not understand Father's actions."

Her mother came over with a tolerant smile. She fussed with Evangeline's curls. "It is not for you to understand. Just know that your father always has the best interests of this family in mind. We all have a duty to the family." Her gaze met Evangeline's evenly. "All of us."

Evangeline swallowed hard, thoroughly chastened. She'd never had friends—not until Albert, if he could be called that. Family was everything. She understood that. But that was precisely the problem.

What sort of family could she have with a man like the duke?

All of the dreams she'd harbored—of marrying for love, of having children, and living a quiet life in the country with her family around her…

She had to bid farewell to that, as well.

Her mother forced a small smile. "I've coddled you too much, I fear. Your father, too."

Evangeline's lips quivered. Was that what this was? Her father and mother seemed to think her a child for wanting a say in her future. "Is it so very wrong to want to be happy?"

"You can be happy as a duchess—"

"I hate being the center of attention," she said, turning away, back toward the window. "I've never wanted to dwell amongst the *ton*. I've only ever wanted one thing."

Love.

The word went unspoken. Her mother would only call her childish again if she spoke of such things.

Her mother sighed. "Dearest, what you and Mr. Foley shared…"

Evangeline stiffened. She could not talk to her mother about Albert just now. Not now when she was about to marry.

"I suspected you might not listen to me," her mother continued. Something in her voice had Evangeline turning to face her.

"Which is why I've arranged for you to meet with your

friend," her mother said, her expression pinched with warning.

Hope had Evangeline straightening away from the window's edge. "Mother, do you mean...?"

Her mother turned away with a sigh and opened the door to say something in a muffled voice. She turned back with the door still partially open. "Don't forget your duty to your family," her mother said sternly. "And for heaven's sake, don't do anything to ruin this gift we've been given."

"What—" Before she could finish, her mother slipped out, and Albert came in.

"Albert." She threw herself into his waiting arms. He held her tight, and when she pulled back, she saw that he was just as distraught as she. His blond hair seemed to have wilted into his eyes, and his eyes looked sunken and hollow. "Oh, Albert. I cannot believe my father denied you."

"Hush, my love, it will be all right." He mustered an encouraging smile. "Your mother wishes for me to calm you—"

"Don't listen to her," Evangeline said.

Even as she said it, her mind filled with her mother's parting words. Her duty to her family.

Her heart sank all over again. Even if Albert wanted to whisk her away to Gretna Green, she could not be so disobedient. Her family's name would never recover from the scandal. And so she wept in Albert's arms as he consoled her.

Some part of her marveled at this scene they were enacting. How very tragic that the first time her love had ever held her in his arms it was on her wedding day. To another man.

"He's horrible." She sniffed as she pulled back. "You know I would never choose him over you."

"For your sake, I hope he is not as cruel as they claim." His mouth was set in a grim line that made her belly tremble.

Cruel? Was that what they said? She'd heard whispers about the duke but knew little for certain.

"If he is unbearable, love, you must tell me." His voice was earnest, his pale eyes bright with affection. "You have only to say the word, my dearest, and I will be there to save you. I will take you away from this fiend who's come between us."

She pulled back, her heart breaking at his determination.

Truthfully, she could not imagine ever harming her family in such a way. She might have been a disappointment to them, but they were the only home she'd ever known.

But for his sake, she nodded. "Yes, Albert."

He turned away from her with one last parting glance.

"And Albert—" she called as he went to slip outside again, their time being so painfully short. "He may claim me as his wife, but he will never have my heart."

The words were mawkish, perhaps, but they needed to be said. For she'd never been more certain of anything.

She'd thought ill of the duke after his abhorrent behavior at the ball, but right now, she despised him with every part of her.

Albert's smile was tremulous, and he turned away with a sad sigh.

Sniffing and swiping away her tears, a few moments later, Evangeline followed in his wake, joining her mother to leave for the church.

The pews of the grand cathedral were full, though Evangeline knew few of the guests aside from her family. It didn't matter. What mattered was the man at the front of the church.

The duke.

Her heart twisted and rebelled as his gaze caught hers. She walked down the aisle, a prisoner on her way to the gallows. That was how it felt, at least.

She was being melodramatic, obviously. She knew that, but she didn't care.

She was an actress, after all. That's what today was. A performance.

A farce.

As she moved down the aisle, her skin burned where the stares fell. Her insides revolted at this display.

She hated it. She'd never wanted it.

Her gaze met his again, so fierce and so smug. The predator who'd caught his prey.

She hated him.

Despite the heat crackling through her at being the center of attention, sheer dread had the blood rushing from her head, leaving her pale and dizzy when she reached his side.

The duke's hand came to her arm, and she flinched. She despised this man with all her heart and soul. But if she didn't want to collapse right here and now…she needed him.

"I've got you, Angel," he said in that low, emotionless voice of his as he steadied her. "You're safe now."

She blinked up at him, her lips parted in surprise. Was that what he thought? She was safe?

Did he think her happy, too?

This fool. This maddening, arrogant, overbearing *fool*.

"It's almost over," he murmured again a little while later as the minister's voice droned on.

Was it? She didn't care. Because for her, the moment this farce ended, the true nightmare would begin.

CHAPTER FIVE

R AFF LEANED BACK in the armchair in his study with a smug smile. His gaze found the clock on the mantel as he tapped his fingers on the desk's edge. He'd waited long enough to claim his prize, hadn't he?

He shoved back from the desk, his smile widening with anticipation.

He'd given Evangeline hours to adjust to her new suite of rooms, her lady's maid and the rest of the servants coming and going from her quarters as she was bathed and readied for him.

And now, at last, it was time.

He stretched his arms overhead as he strode toward the stairs. This wait had felt like an eternity. But then again, he'd never had to wait before. Not for anything. Not even the dukedom, thanks to his father's early demise.

He'd had the world at his fingertips ever since. Not a bad way to live, really. And soon enough, his bride would come to see all the perks that came with being a duchess.

He grinned as he headed up the stairs toward her rooms. At last, the time had come. His little dove must be beside herself with nerves. She'd been frightened all day, poor angel. His friends had taunted him endlessly about his bride-to-be's pallor after the fact. At their wedding breakfast afterward, Malcolm, Benedict, and Hayden had taken every opportunity to point out that she wasn't eating.

Of course, she hadn't been eating. Bloody hell, she'd barely been standing on her own two feet. But it was merely nerves. Her mother had said as much when he'd gone to Evangeline's side to see if he might be of assistance.

Her mother had assured him she'd be well just as soon as all the fuss was behind her.

His new wife, meanwhile, had merely blinked up at him as though he were a stranger. Which, to be fair, he supposed he was.

He reached for the doorknob. But he'd not be a stranger for long. After tonight, they'd be intimately acquainted.

And once she was with child, they could go their separate ways if their feelings were not compatible.

He felt confident that a young lady so well-bred as Evangeline would have no issue adapting to the running of a household such as his.

Yes, all was going exactly to plan. And all would be well indeed once he'd taken her to bed and helped her past her silly fears.

He knocked once but did not wait for an answer before striding into the room.

He stopped short at the sight before him.

His angel. He'd never been more aware of her ethereal charms than he was right at this moment. With her long, pale blonde locks hanging down her back, her slim frame and lush curves silhouetted through the thin fabric of her night rail by the flames flickering in the fireplace behind her.

She was exceptional.

She was exquisite.

And she was his.

A surge of triumph had him striding toward her, slowing only when he saw her stiffen. Her features were cast in shadow, but he did not need to read her expression to know she was terrified.

Poor little dove had been scared witless all day.

"You can relax, Angel," he said in a voice as soothing as he could manage, considering the way he strained against his breeches.

Reach for her. Take her. Make her yours.

He gritted his teeth against his baser urges. She was a virgin, of course. But the fact had never been so painfully evident as it was right now as she gazed up at him from wide, innocent eyes, her full lips parted in a way that was so unknowingly provocative it sent a surge of heat straight down to his groin.

"Why do you keep calling me that, Your Grace?" Her voice was soft.

Everything about her was soft. Inviting. So feminine and delicate, it made his hands twitch with the effort to keep from touching her.

He would eventually, of course, but he'd put her at ease first. It was the least he could do as a considerate husband.

Husband. The word made his insides twist oddly, trying to digest this new information. Him. A husband.

"Why do I call you Angel?" he asked as he moved toward the tray he'd had the servants leave for them. He opened the bottle of wine and poured them both a glass.

"Yes, Your Grace."

Your Grace. He smiled down at the glasses in his hands before turning to offer her one. "I am your husband now, Angel. You may call me William, if you'd like. Or Raff." His tongue felt unexpectedly thick under her watchful gaze. "My friends call me Raff."

Her gaze dropped to the glass of wine he was still holding out to her. "I don't imbibe, Your Grace."

He stilled. Your Grace again. Was it just nerves, or was she trying to keep him at arm's length?

But one look at those big eyes, those soft lips…

No. This sweet thing wasn't cold, just shy. Her father had said as much time and again as they'd worked out the final contract. The memory of that meeting had his hand dropping along with his smile, and he set the wine glass down on the mantel beside her.

The move had him close enough now that he could smell the scented oil from the bath she'd taken. It mixed with her natural feminine scent and went right to his head, more heady than any wine could hope to be.

"Do you not like the term of endearment?" he asked.

"I do not understand it," she said.

He was close enough to see the flutter of her pulse at the base of her neck. Poor little lamb was so frightened. "What's not to understand?" he said, laughter edging his words. "Your beauty is not of this world, and your temperament..." He allowed his words to fade off, giving her a gentle smile.

"What do you know of my temperament?" she asked.

Again, so mild, so sweet, and yet...

She shifted, and her eyes glinted with firelight. For a moment, it seemed like anger.

No...fury.

He blinked, and it was gone. She was once more a docile lamb. He drew in a deep breath. He was meant to be the steady hand here. She was an inexperienced virgin, after all. It was only natural she would be on guard.

"The first time I saw you, I was struck by your unworldly beauty. Then, when I spoke to your father, he called you Angie." He smiled. "I thought Angel made for a fitting term of endearment, but if you'd prefer—"

"Do not call me Angie." Her voice was unexpectedly hard.

He blinked. "Right. Very well."

"Angel is fine," she continued. "But I'm afraid you'll be disappointed."

His shoulders sank as his muscles relaxed. Ah, so that was it. "You could never disappoint me, Angel."

Her brows hitched up slightly. "You seem awfully certain."

Oh himself? Or of her?

Either way... He moved closer. "I am known for being a decisive man, Evangeline. I know what I like, and once I have my heart on something, I never waver. You should know this about me."

Her chin came up a little higher. "Oh yes. I am well aware of your tendency to take what you believe to be yours."

His head jerked back at the sudden change in her tone. It wasn't just hard. It was frigid.

He narrowed his eyes to peer at her. But that couldn't be right.

He shifted toward the fire, changing the angle at which he viewed her for a better look at her.

Bloody hell, she was obscenely gorgeous. She was temptation itself standing before him with those curves and those lips, her eyes glittering like diamonds in the firelight, her cheeks flushed with…

With what?

By the way her chest heaved, making her lovely breasts rise and fall, he'd have said passion. Excitement. But that didn't explain the way her eyes hardened as she met his gaze.

"Evangeline," he said slowly. "It would be quite understandable if you have been overwhelmed by the excitement of the day."

She made a soft noise that could only be described as a snort of disdain.

And then, to his amazement, she reached for the glass of wine and tossed it back in one go. "Perhaps you were right," she said as she set it back down with a loud clink. "Perhaps I do need some fortification for what is to come."

As she said it, she slid a narrowed glare toward the bed as if the piece of furniture had just insulted her family.

For the first time in his life, Raff was speechless.

More than that, he was thoroughly confused. What had happened to the soft, sweet, docile little angel he'd met on the dance floor? The one so overcome with intimidation in his presence, she could hardly string two words together.

But as he watched her, he saw that fire grow in her eyes until it was blazing beyond reason.

It was fetching, to be honest. It turned her from a pretty angel to an awe-inspiring goddess. But it had his own blood boiling with anger in return.

This was his home. She was his wife. They hadn't even lain together yet, and she was turning on him like some nagging fishwife?

That was *not* how this night would go.

He set his own glass down, slower but with no less force. "Are you trying to tell me that you did not wish for this marriage?"

Her lips parted, those sparkling blue eyes widened. For a moment, he thought she might cry, and he braced himself for it.

Instead, she laughed. It was a bitter sound and not at all pleasing to the ear. "Is that an honest question?" she asked. "It cannot be. You must know I did not want this. I made that clear from the start. Surely my father told you of my feelings on the matter."

He stared at her as his stomach churned.

Bloody hell.

She was in earnest. Her father had said as much the first time he'd paid a visit, but he hadn't believed him. And the second time he'd come to see her father, a proposition and contract in hand, her father hadn't deigned to mention again that his daughter was opposed to the idea.

And so he'd thought…

He'd just assumed…

Oh, Christ. What a mess.

She spread her arms wide, and once more, he was reminded of an angel—an avenging angel—a fiery paragon of virtue sent to strike down powerful men like him.

"You knew I did not want to marry you, and yet you claimed me anyway. Why? I cannot understand it," she said.

Her pretty lips pushed out in a pout that was at once childish and absurdly tempting.

He cursed under his breath as his cock strained toward her, as if those lips were puckering up to take his hard staff into her mouth.

His cock couldn't have been more wrong.

Raff's nostrils flared. His hands clenched. Never in his life had he been chastened in such a manner, and certainly not by some young lady who knew nothing of the world or his responsibilities.

"I suppose you wanted my dowry, is that it?" she continued.

Those words were a douse of cold water on the flames of his rising anger.

For a moment, all he could do was stare at the girl as the truth settled like a cold weight in his bones.

She didn't know.

Her feckless, weak father hadn't told her the truth.

It was on the tip of his tongue to tell her now. He hadn't received a bloody shilling of her dowry because her dowry didn't exist. Her father had lost it all. Gambled it away, along with everything else he'd inherited.

The old coot had planned on marrying her off to one of his friends he owed money to. He'd told Raff as much plainly.

Did she truly not know that? Had she not at least guessed?

He raked a hand through his hair. He couldn't be the one to tell her. Not now when she was already distraught.

Besides, she likely wouldn't even believe him.

She turned away from him with a huff, and despite his irritation, he watched those glorious, sumptuous breasts rise and fall as she took a deep breath. From this view, he could see the dark shadow of her nipples as they pressed against the fine fabric.

His gaze dropped of its own accord, taking in the swell of her bottom, and as she shifted to face him—

He just barely swallowed a groan.

There was that dark V between her thighs. The hint of salvation for his poor, straining erection.

Her sharp inhale had his gaze lifting, and her cheeks caught fire. They were so red it looked painful. Quickly, she covered her breasts with one arm, her free hand covering her mound as she whimpered.

"Bloody hell," he muttered. "You're my wife, Evangeline."

She visibly swallowed, and her earlier anger seemed to give way to fear.

A sick twisting sensation in his gut had him backing up a step. He'd bedded countless women over the years, but never once had a lady cowered before him.

Never once had she been unwilling.

His lip curled up in a sneer. "Rest easy, Angel. I am not about to force myself on you."

"Why not?" she shot back. "It's your right. And we both know you have no qualms about claiming whatever it is you want, regardless of who gets hurt."

Who gets hurt?

She truly believed she was some sort of victim here. The thought struck him like a blow and then settled under his skin, into his blood.

"I made you a *duchess*." It came out louder than intended. Despite all his best efforts, the smiling charming facade slipped. He gestured around the opulent suite of rooms to the grand townhouse that lay beyond. "I took you away from a fate that was beneath you—"

"How do you know what my fate might have been?" Her chest was heaving now, and her voice was breathless with emotion. "How do you know what you have kept me from?"

He stared with an open mouth as his mind struggled to catch up.

It was on the tip of his tongue to inform her exactly what he'd kept her from. Being sold off to pay her father's debts to someone too old, too cruel, too poor...

But once again, he couldn't bring himself to say it.

He might be a callous, presumptuous arse, but he wasn't about to kick the girl when she was down. He wasn't *that* low. The girl was clearly heartbroken, after all, and—

A new realization stole the air from his lungs as surely as a punch to the gut.

She was *heartbroken*.

"You had another suitor." It wasn't a question.

She didn't deny it, just looked away toward the fire. But her sadness spoke for her.

It couldn't have been one of her father's wealthy friends. Her father wouldn't have been so eager to leap on Raff's offer to pay off his debts if his daughter truly wished to marry another man of wealth who could save them.

Not even her poor excuse for a father would be so cruel.

He crossed his arms and leaned back to study her. "Who is it?"

She did not feign ignorance. Instead, her chin came up, and her eyes glinted with anger. "That is none of your concern."

"You are my wife, which means you are my concern. *All* of you." His gaze raked over her. His jaw worked as he strove for calm, but possessive jealousy had his heart hammering in his chest. "Evangeline, tell me now. Have you let another man touch you—"

"No!" She fairly shouted it. So quickly and with such horror, he did not doubt her word.

"That is what I meant." Her lips quivered for a moment before she tilted her chin up in defiance. "You may have power over my body, Your Grace. But you will never have my heart. That belongs to another."

"Your heart?" He couldn't keep the mockery from his voice. "What use do I have for your heart?"

Disdain flashed in her eyes before she looked away from him.

A muscle ticked in his jaw. Wonderful. His new wife was a romantic nitwit and, apparently, given to mawkish displays of emotion as well.

"That was quite the speech," he said, his voice low and sharp with anger. Indeed, it had sounded like a speech she'd rehearsed. While he'd been biding his time waiting to take her to bed, she'd been rehearsing her rejection.

She'd been thinking about some other man.

His hands clenched and unclenched at his sides. "Now tell me, who do you pine for, *wife?*"

She wet her lips, the only sign of nerves as she dropped her gaze. "That is none of your concern," she said again.

"None of my *concern*?"

She stiffened at the cold rage in his voice.

"You are my mine now, Evangeline. You are my concern. You are mine to care for, mine to protect. You are *mine*."

He took a step back, trying to regain his composure. Trying to regain the use of his mind—difficult to do when she was striking such an erotic picture in front of the fire.

The bed was right there. All he needed to do was pick her up and throw her down. His jaw clenched at the thought of turning her anger into passion.

He could hitch up the skirt of her night rail and touch her, tease her. He knew how to bring a woman pleasure, and the thought of erasing that accusatory look in her eyes and replacing it with dazed, sensual pleasure…

It was tempting. And she'd allow it because, as she said, it was his right.

Bloody hell, he didn't need her to tell him his rights. He was master of this house.

He stalked closer. He was master of *her*.

He reached out and cupped her cheek. She flinched even though his touch was as achingly gentle as if he were touching glass. She felt just as smooth. But where glass was cold, her skin seemed to flicker and glow with heat.

Her lips parted as her gaze met his and held.

He shifted closer, just enough so the tips of those high, round breasts rubbed against his chest. He ached to get even closer, but he held still, watching her eyes widen and darken.

She felt it. His Evangeline might look like an angel, but she was no saint.

She had a temper he hadn't expected. Bravery, too, if he were being honest. And the way her eyes darkened, the way her nipples hardened as he leaned in closer…

Oh no, she was no saint. She wanted him physically, even if she wouldn't admit it.

She had to. Because lust had wrapped around him like a second skin, just as it had the very first time he'd laid eyes on her. He wanted her even more now than when he'd held her in his arms on the dance floor.

The fire in her eyes only made her that much more appealing.

"You think I wanted you for your dowry," he said, his voice surprisingly calm despite the storm inside him.

She blinked, her gaze focusing. "Didn't you?"

He leaned in closer until her breath fanned across his cheek, a harsh whisper in his ear.

"I didn't want you for your dowry, Evangeline, nor your family connections." He pulled back so he could meet her gaze. "Make no mistake. There is an endless supply of young, pretty, wealthy, titled ladies in this world who would have fought to the death to be my bride."

Her eyes flared with emotion. Anger, no doubt.

It was likely beyond crass to point out how many other women he might have had. How many women he had enjoyed. He cut himself off before he could offend her further by telling her how many women he planned to enjoy once she was round with his child.

"So? Why did you not marry one of those foolish girls instead?" She arched her brows in defiance, and for just a moment, his anger was rivaled by a surge of amazement at her reckless courage.

If he were a different man, a crueler man, he'd have had her over his knee by now and taught her what it meant to have a master. Then he'd flip her over onto her back and show her what it meant to be the possession of a man such as him.

He moved in closer, finally giving in to the urge to tug her close, so the hard length of his erection pressed against her soft belly.

Her gasp rent the air, and he gave her a humorless smirk in response. "I chose you because I want you, Evangeline. And you were right." His lips curved up in a humorless smile. "I always get what I want."

CHAPTER SIX

S HE OUGHT TO be terrified.

And she *was* scared. Her heart was hammering so wildly because she was afraid.

That was the only reason.

Though, as she leaned in slightly, curious at the hard *thing* that was jabbing her in the belly, she realized that perhaps she ought to be more frightened than she was.

But despite the duke's hard smile as he glared down at her, despite the way he held her tight and the obscene way he was shoving himself into her, she wasn't entirely scared.

She was also…hot. Disturbingly so. Her limbs were heavy, and her blood too warm as their breathing mingled, and she waited for him to act.

He wouldn't force himself on her. She knew that. He was taunting her, trying to demonstrate his power, but there was no real cruelty in his eyes. And he'd been in earnest before when he'd said he wouldn't force her.

The thought of taking her against her will seemed to have filled him with disgust, by the looks of it.

That was why she wasn't as afraid as she ought to be, she supposed.

For all his snarling and growls, for all his high-handed statements about how lucky she ought to consider herself, he was not going to have his way with her.

She pulled back, testing this theory. After a brief resistance, he let her go.

And now they were both breathing heavily as if they'd come to blows and not just stood in one another's arms.

She turned away toward the fire as she struggled for composure.

Albert. She needed to remember Albert. She'd given him her heart; it was his forever. But the reality of her new situation was impossible to avoid now that she was here, in *his* home, as his wife, surrounded by his servants.

This was her life now. She was a wife. And perhaps someday, she'd be a mother.

The thought was the only bright spot in the darkened sky that had been hovering over her for the past fortnight.

Albert would come for her if this life was unbearably awful.

But could she do that to her parents? Could she cast them in scandal and force Albert to live outside of society if she were deemed a traitorous wife? No, of course, she could not.

Her mother was right. It was time to grow up. Time to accept her fate.

Her limbs stiff with determination, she awkwardly moved past him to the bed.

"What are you doing?" he snapped.

She assumed it was obvious as she climbed up on the high bed with as much grace as she could muster.

Now that her anger was fading, her hands began to tremble with what was about to occur. Her mother had told her what to expect and what was expected of her. To lie there. That was all she must do. Lie there and suffer in silence.

With a deep breath, she lay back against the pillows, shutting her eyes tight, the crackle of the fire the only sound in this overwhelmingly large room with its excessively large bed and the irritatingly large duke.

The bed sank with a creak, but she did not open her eyes to

see him.

"Evangeline." His voice sounded too loud in this silence. Too loud and too…practical. There was no hint of that angry growl or the passion in his voice when he'd held her close.

She peeked at him through one eye.

"What are you doing?" He looked genuinely perplexed and more than a little irritated.

She let out a long exhale as she shut her eyes. "My wifely duty."

"Your—"

It sounded as though he choked on the word, and he didn't finish his thought. The bed jostled again as he came up to join her.

She waited for the feel of his heavy weight crushing her, but what she got was…a gentle stroke of his hand over her cheek.

Her eyes flew open, and that was a mistake. For he was close. Closer than he'd ever been. Close enough that she could see the gold flecks in his dark eyes and the light stubble that covered his jawline. Close enough that she could taste the wine on his breath and feel the heat from his skin as he hovered over her.

Hovering, but not touching.

"I know I don't exactly have a decent reputation among society," he said softly, his voice oddly soothing, even as it stirred a curious sensation deep in her belly with its low rumble. "And for good reason," he said. "I am not a good man. I gamble, I drink, and I've never been faithful to any woman." His gaze met hers. "And I never plan to be."

Her lips parted as the air rushed out of her lungs.

His eyes glinted dangerously as his fingers continued to stroke her cheek, her jaw, her hair. It was the sort of touch one might use to calm a fretful child, and it confused her, mentally and physically.

He was touching her tenderly while informing her that he would not be a faithful husband. He was caressing her sweetly after telling her that he'd only married her to have his way with her.

She frowned. She did not understand him at all.

"I would obviously not have told you that last fact," he said, his tone growing lazy as his hand tangled in her hair, stroking her scalp and sending a cascade of unexpected sensations down her spine. "I wouldn't have told you about my plans to continue taking mistresses and enjoying whores, except that you clearly wish for abject honesty between us."

His gaze clashed with hers again, and the ferocity there stole her breath.

"So let me be clear, Angel. I don't care who owns your heart. I don't care what you do with that overactive mind of yours. But your body is mine." His gaze seared her with its fire. "As your husband, I have claim to that. Do you understand?"

She gave a short nod, her heart fluttering frantically. He wasn't holding her down in any way, but she was trapped. Captive.

At his mercy.

"But *your* body does not belong to me, is that it?" She heard her voice, heard her words, but they were not what she'd meant to say.

She almost sounded...jealous. But that wasn't right. She didn't want his body. She didn't want *him* at all.

His lips curved up on one side. "It's yours if you lay claim to it, love."

A shiver raced through her and made her tremble. He made a sweet shushing sound as if to soothe her as he leaned over her, burrowing his face in the crook between her head and her shoulder and trailing the softest of kisses along skin she hadn't realized was so very sensitive.

She gasped at the feel of his lips moving lightly over the flesh beneath her ear. So lightly, it made something deep inside her ache at the gentleness of it, so at odds with the firm voice and fiery glare.

Her back arched slightly, involuntarily, like her body was

asking for something, and she didn't know what.

She could feel his smile against her neck as he continued in low, soothing tones.

"That is the deal we shall strike between us here tonight, Angel. Here and now, let us strike a bargain, so we might live harmoniously, hmm?"

She couldn't protest even if she wanted to. Her mouth had gone dry, and her lungs refused to draw in air as his lips wandered over her jaw and chin, his stubble making her shiver whenever it brushed against her soft skin.

"Unfair as it might be, I must insist that you keep your body for me alone—I cannot risk you bearing another man's child, after all," he said. "Responsibilities to the dukedom, and all that."

How was he talking? She could only barely keep up with him as he continued his light caresses and gentle kissing.

"And if you decide you wish to take upon the task of keeping me sated in bed," he continued. "If you decide you'd like to be the woman who fulfills all my needs—" He pulled back to look down at her with eyes dark with desire. "Of which there are many, I should warn you." He leaned down and grazed his lips over hers in a soft, sweet kiss that made her gasp for air. "Why then, all you have to do is claim your place in my bed, and I shall be faithful as well. Is that fair?"

She found herself nodding dazedly. It sounded reasonable.

He would be faithful if she wanted him to be.

But she wouldn't want him to be.

And she *would* be faithful. There was nothing to debate there. She'd already made that promise to God in church that very morning.

"Say yes if you understand," he said.

"Yes," she whispered.

He cut the word off with another kiss, harder this time as though he were sealing the vow with his lips. His lips crushed hers, firm and hot as a brand. She stiffened at the force of it, but he eased the force of his kiss quickly. Then he was moving his mouth over hers, slowly at first, and then with more insistence. His lips were hot and sure, teasing hers, prodding hers. It felt like they were asking a question.

The kisses were leisurely but incessant, unyielding in their persistence, and the overall effect was confusing. His warmth was spreading over her, through her, surrounding her. Her hands lay at her sides, but her fingers moved restlessly over the duvet as his gentle assault made her thoughts scatter with each new touch.

When she parted her lips for air, his tongue flicked out and touched her lower lip. She gasped and then felt his answering smile against her mouth.

She couldn't breathe. The way he was kissing her now, it was…it was surely wrong. It was messy and wild.

His mouth was open against hers, hot and wet and slanting over hers for more access.

His kiss was wild, and it made *her* feel wild, like her body was out of her control. Each time his lips clung to hers, her body moved to answer. Like a call and an echo, she found herself kissing him back without meaning to. Her body was shifting and swaying along with his as his tongue teased her lips wider, the heat of his mouth making her forget that this wasn't what she wanted.

What she wanted was…

More.

Her thoughts had abandoned her. Her body was in control now, and it was asking for more. More heat. More friction. More touching. More tasting.

Her hands came up to touch him, a light touch first to his hard chest and then lower, stopping when he groaned into her mouth before plunging his tongue inside her, stroking hers with a familiarity that made her whimper.

He pulled back, his breathing heavy as her chest rose and fell. She struggled to get air. Her head was spinning, and his darkened gaze made her skin burn wherever it fell.

His gaze roamed over her, and this time, she didn't try to

cover herself, clutching the covers beneath her instead.

She was a wife now. This was her duty.

That was what she told herself. But when his gaze stopped at her breasts, she couldn't quite lie still. Her nipples chafed against the material, and her skin was impossibly hot.

She waited for him to order her to undress.

Or perhaps he would do it?

She trembled beneath him as she waited.

He reached out and trailed one finger down the length of her neck, over her collarbone, and over the curve of her right breast. He stopped at the hardened tip that even she could see poking up through her clothing.

"So beautiful, Angel." He traced the tip of her breast, circling it teasingly with his finger. The touch was so light, so gentle, she found herself arching up again with a sound that made her wince.

She sounded needy. Desperate.

What was happening to her?

Was this normal?

Her mother hadn't mentioned anything about tracing her breasts through her clothing. In fact, none of this was what she'd expected.

He murmured something that sounded like, "One taste," and then he was leaning over her, his hot mouth clamping over her breast and—

"Oh!" She clapped a hand over her mouth as he suckled her nipple through the thin fabric, the wet heat sending a flare of warmth from her breasts straight down to her core. A moan slipped out from behind her hand as that heat grew and pooled between her thighs.

What was happening?

What wickedness was he doing to her?

Quite without thinking, she dropped her hand from her mouth. She meant to push his shoulder, to unlatch his hot mouth from her breast, but then she found her hand on the back of his head instead. Her fingers buried in his thick dark hair, and in her addled state, she couldn't say if she were trying to tear his head away or hold him closer.

His low chuckle as he cupped her breasts together and burrowed his face between them seemed to say that he knew.

He moved his head back and forth, his mouth hot and insistent against the sensitive skin of her nipples.

Her breathing was fast, and odd little whimpers kept escaping her. She couldn't lie still no matter how hard she tried. She kept arching, and then her hips would buck upward. There was an ache there that she could not name, could not understand. But it was growing more painful with his every kiss.

Was this the pain her mother referred to?

She wanted to ask him.

She had no idea how to ask him.

He seemed to understand what was happening, though, because he let one hand slide from her breasts over her belly until it reached that hot, aching spot between her thighs. Still touching her over her clothes, he pressed a firm hand between her legs, cupping her with thick, demanding fingers.

With a shout, her hips rose up. He wasn't hurting her, but the feel of anyone touching her there was so new, and so…so…

Another whimper escaped as her legs parted to give him more access. His touch was easing the ache and making it worse all at once. His mouth moved back to hers, and he swallowed her whimpers before kissing her neck. "Easy, Angel. I have you."

I have you. There it was again. That reassurance that was at once heartwarming and infuriating.

He pulled back to gaze down at her, and his eyes were so dark, she wondered if one could get lost in them.

"Now," he said, his voice back to the way it had been before when he'd first approached. So practical and low and…unmoved. His lips quirked up in a small smirk that made her gut tighten. "Tell me, Angel. Do you want me to claim you as my wife?"

It was the arrogance in his voice that had her lips clamping shut and her mind racing back into action.

He was so sure of himself. So sure of her.

Through clenched teeth, she said, "I will do my duty."

His eyes flared with temper, and his eyes narrowed dangerously. "Your duty."

She squeezed her eyes shut once more, and she spread her legs as her mother had told her to do. "Do what you must."

A second passed. Then two.

When the bed jostled, she opened her eyes in confusion. "Where are you going?" she asked as he adjusted his pants and turned toward the fire.

When he turned back, his eyes were dancing with the reflection of the flames. He looked like the very devil himself.

"Despite what rumors you might have heard about me, Angel, I am not going to steal your virginity. Even if it is mine for the taking."

She blinked, her lips parting, that ache between her thighs turning to a pulsing pain that left her as befuddled as his words. "You're not?"

"No." He straightened his shirt as he walked around the other side of the bed, toward the door leading to his room. "I won't steal it." He paused at the side of the bed, his gaze sweeping over her with such smug arrogance she felt a wave of hatred in its wake. "I will not have to steal it." His gaze darted up to meet hers. "You'll give it to me willingly."

She gasped, opening her mouth to protest.

He leaned over her with a smile and kissed her before she could argue. When he pulled back, his eyes were hard. "Trust me, Angel. When the time is right, you're going to beg me to take it."

CHAPTER SEVEN

R AFF WAS IN the library when the cloudy sky finally opened, letting out a torrent of rain as it had been promising to do all morning.

Well, this was just wonderful.

He kicked his feet up onto the edge of the settee as he tried to focus on the book in his hand. It wasn't working.

He was restless and had been all day.

After a night spent lying awake trying not to think about his tempting bride and her delicious body in the other room, he'd come downstairs to find her. Everywhere he turned, he kept running into her.

She was never alone. It seemed his household staff was just as smitten with his new bride as he'd been that first night he'd met her. His housekeeper had been fussing over her at the breakfast table, and then the butler had been lecturing her about the history of the estate, and then he'd found her with a maid, who was explaining what exactly she did for his house.

During each interaction, Evangeline had been the picture of kindness and propriety. The perfect duchess, just as he'd known she would be.

He scoffed aloud as he reached for his snifter of brandy.

Oh, yes, he'd guessed correctly that she'd play the part of duchess well. He just hadn't understood that her prim and proper young lady routine was all a façade. Beneath that she was—well, she was still a sweetheart, he suspected. Innocent, sheltered, and too romantic for her own good, perhaps. But from what he'd seen today, she was also kindhearted and gentle.

To everyone but him.

No, he was the only one to see that fiery temper she hid so well.

He frowned down at the contents of the glass as his cock stirred to life all over again. His jaw clenched. One would think a man would stop being so bloody attracted to a woman after she all but accused him of kidnapping her and ruining her life.

But instead, that fire in her had lit one of his own, and he couldn't stop picturing her face as she'd lain below him, her perfect face aglow from the light of the fire and her eyes flickering with life.

With *passion*.

He swallowed hard as he adjusted himself. And the way she'd writhed beneath him. The way she'd kissed him back, unskilled but fervent. Almost desperate. Those sweet little whimpers and gasps…

He could imagine far too well just what it would be like to take her.

And that was precisely why he'd made that bargain with her. If she wanted to be the one in his bed, he knew without a doubt that she'd more than satisfy him.

In fact, he had a suspicion that once he tasted her sweet virgin body, he'd be ruined for all others.

Hell. He dropped his head back. That was a depressing thought.

"Oh. Pardon me." That soft voice that had been haunting his thoughts all day had him lifting his head with a jerk to find Evangeline hovering just inside the library's doorway.

She lifted her skirts to turn back around, her head dipping to avoid his gaze. "I did not realize you were in here. I would not wish to disturb you."

"Wait."

She stilled.

He swallowed. It wasn't as though he'd actively been steering clear of Evangeline today. It was just that the sight of her was sheer torment. He was supposed to be fucking her senseless during this respite from London. He was supposed to be siring an heir while relieving this absurd desire that had kept him in its clutches since the moment he'd seen her descending the staircase at her parents' ball.

And yet, here he was. Hard as wood, his ballocks aching for relief. And all because he was too bloody noble to just go ahead and take what was his.

She stood there for an age, silent as he was, as they regarded one another.

This was ridiculous. They were meant to spend their lives together. They couldn't avoid each other forever. And besides, if he meant to make her beg for it, he'd need another opportunity to get close.

Leaning forward, he gave her what he hoped was a reassuring smile. "Come," he said, gesturing to the seat beside him before the fire. "Join me."

"Oh, that's quite all right, I'll just—"

"Angel, this house is monstrously large and ridiculously old. Which means just about every room is drafty at this time of year." He nodded toward the window where rain pelted the glass. "Add in this weather, and you're guaranteed to freeze if you're anywhere but here."

He nodded toward the roaring fire warming the small, cozy room.

"Very well," she said softly, stepping past him to perch her perfect little bottom on the seat beside him.

And then she went quiet, her gaze dropping to her hands.

She was gorgeous. Her hair was piled atop her head like some silken crown, a few soft tendrils framing her heart-shaped face and drawing his gaze to her long, slender neck.

Once more, she looked like an angel. *His* angel. The woman he'd thought he was marrying.

Her silence grated at him. She'd had no trouble speaking the night before. In fact, she'd been just fine throwing out accusations and standing up to him in a way no one ever had before, aside from his closest friends.

He winced at the mere thought of what Hayden, Benedict, and Malcolm would say if they knew that he hadn't managed to bed his own wife on his wedding night. He'd never hear the end of it.

He tapped his fingers against the front of his book as he watched her. Her words from the night before kept coming back to him. Two phrases in particular.

You don't know me at all.

That one stuck in his craw because…

Well, because she was right. He'd been wrong. He'd thought he'd had her pegged, but he hadn't bothered to look beyond the perfect face and heavenly body.

You will never have my heart. That belongs to another.

That one had his muscles tensing with fury even now. He wasn't one to share. Not anything. Certainly not his wife. And while he did not think her so stupid as to try and cuckold him— she likely wouldn't have told him about the other man if she'd had plans of sneaking off to see her beloved—the fact that she was pining for another man while wearing his ring had his jaw clenched tight.

"Did Mrs. Harper give you a tour of the estate?" he asked.

"Yes, Your Grace," she said quickly. Her demeanor was once more that of the dutiful little darling.

What an odd little riddle he'd gotten himself with this one.

"And are your rooms to your liking?" he continued. Even he could hear the impatience that edged his voice, much as he tried to stifle it.

"Indeed, Your Grace."

"I thought I told you to stop calling me that," he bit out

through clenched teeth.

It was one thing to have a wife who despised him. It was quite another to have a wife who treated him like he was nothing more than his title.

"My apologies, Your—er, William."

He winced, and he was fairly certain she did as well. His first name sounded awkward coming from her. Probably because he'd forced her into this new intimacy.

Bloody hell, he couldn't seem to stop making a mess of this entire situation.

He scratched at his jaw as he tried to figure out how to salvage this. "So, which is it then?" he asked suddenly.

Her head came up with a start. "Pardon me?"

Such sweet, guileless eyes. He met her gaze evenly. "Which is it today? Are you the meek, obedient, easily intimidated young lady I met at the ball, or are you the fiery avenging angel I had the pleasure of kissing last night?"

Her eyes widened, and her cheeks went scarlet. "I-I—" She swallowed. "I was never intimidated."

It was so not at all the response he'd expected, and he shocked them both with a loud bark of laughter.

Her lips twitched with an uncertain smile in return.

"You weren't intimidated," he said, leaning forward. "Then why couldn't you meet my eyes or say more than two words at a time?"

She wet her lips as she gave a delicate shrug. "I wasn't intimidated, just shy."

"Shy." The word sounded strange on his tongue. His brows drew together. "Truly?"

She nodded, her gaze dropping once more. "Yes, Your Grace."

He sighed.

She flinched.

He sank back with another loud exhale.

"I don't enjoy being the center of attention, and I've never been terribly good at speaking to anyone outside of my family."

He regarded her for a long moment. She was telling the truth, that much was clear. "You seemed to do just fine last night."

Her cheeks turned impossibly red as she dipped her head. "I was emotional, Your Grace."

"You were angry," he amended.

"Yes, Your Grace."

He couldn't stop staring at her profile, even though he knew quite well it made her uncomfortable. But he had this notion that he was only now starting to really see her.

And he wanted to see all of her.

She was his wife, after all. He ought to know who he'd married.

She kept her head dipped down, but her fingers fidgeted with her skirts, the only telltale sign of her discomfort. "Your Grace, you should know… That is… I will do my duties as a duchess to the best of my abilities. But when it comes to entertaining…" Her throat worked as she swallowed.

For a moment, he actually pitied her. The fear that flickered across her features was more pronounced now than when she'd thought he was going to ravish her the night before.

"I will do my best," she finally finished.

"Well, fortunately for you, I don't enjoy entertaining," he said.

Her gaze lifted, and her blue eyes sparkled with hope. "Truly?"

He gave a short grunt of acknowledgment. Not really. He enjoyed throwing parties for his friends. But those parties were hardly the sort he'd expect any wife to condone, let alone partake in.

But he was pleased to see that his answer had her shoulders sinking with relief.

"Was that why you did not wish to be a duchess?" he asked. "You ought to have told me."

"You ought to have asked," she shot back.

Her head dipped again, and she caught her lower lip between her teeth.

He chuckled. "Do you know, I think I prefer this feisty little angel to that docile girl I thought I'd married."

"You do?" She sounded so shocked it made his heart do an odd sort of contraction in his chest.

"You didn't answer," he said. "Were the responsibilities of a duchess what made you so vehemently opposed to marriage?"

Or was it me?

The thought didn't sit well. No one had ever rejected him before. It left him with questions and more than a little confusion.

She looked away. "That was part of it."

He knew instantly what she meant, and his gut gave a sharp tug. "Ah, yes, the one who holds your heart," he said blandly.

He watched those perfect tits rise and fall as she took a deep breath. Now that he knew how perfect they felt in his hands, it was painful to sit here with his hands at his sides.

Her silence was another form of torture. He didn't want to witness her pining for another.

"Did he ever fuck you?" he asked.

Her head whipped around as she gasped. "Of course not," she said, so prim and proper, it had a laugh threatening to rise up in him. "I already told you that. Do you doubt my virtue?"

He shook his head, but he had to swallow a laugh before he could murmur, "Of course not. My apologies."

"And that language, Your Grace," she continued as if he hadn't spoken, a huff of indignation in her voice.

Such a prudish little thing. Except for when she was arching up, silently begging him for more. He grinned at the memory of her hands in his hair, clutching him to her tits as he'd teased those taut little nipples.

That fiery, wanton lady was nowhere to be seen just now. She was sitting with her back straight and her knees pressed together, her hands clasped tight. "I do not wish to speak of him, Your Grace. I have said my vows before God, and while I will always have affection for him, I am married to you now. I understand that."

Her words were meant to reassure him, and yet they left him even more restless, and the taste on his tongue was decidedly bitter. She would resign herself to being with him instead of the man she truly wanted. That was what she meant.

But she hadn't been thinking of anyone but Raff last night. The thought was mildly comforting.

She hadn't wanted anyone but him.

Evangeline shifted restlessly. "I should go back to my rooms, Your Grace—"

"You'll stay," he said, his tone too curt. He inhaled deeply and softened his voice. "And I do wish you'd stop calling me Your Grace. You don't have to call me William, if that is too intimate, but don't call me by my title. Please."

He couldn't quite meet her curious gaze. It was too depressing by far to have his wife call him that. He couldn't explain why. This house had never been a home, and he'd never had a family—not even when his parents were alive—but he supposed some part of him had thought that taking a wife would change that, at least to some extent.

Having her here in this cold, unwelcoming house that felt like a foreign residence, hearing her call him by his title was just…it was just *wrong*. He wearily rubbed his gritty eyes and sighed. "Anything else but that, Angel."

A long pause followed, and he felt her studying him as he'd done to her.

"Very well…*Devil*." Her sly glance in his direction turned his chuckle into a loud laugh.

"Ah," he said, still grinning. "So you do have a sense of humor, after all."

She didn't respond, but he saw her lips curve up in a reluctant smile. It was small, and it was wary, and it was so beautiful, he ached to see more of her smiles. He wanted to see what her eyes looked like when they were lit with joy, not anger.

"You were right," he said, so suddenly, her eyes widened in shock.

She blinked. "About?"

He cleared his throat and glanced away. "I ought to have taken the time to get to know you. I should have taken your wishes into consideration." It was on the tip of his tongue to tell her why he hadn't believed her father. But much as his pride wished to rationalize his actions, he didn't wish to upset her.

He also couldn't bring himself to apologize. Mainly because he was a duke. He did not apologize. Also, because...truthfully, he wasn't entirely certain he'd done her wrong.

He might have gone about it badly, but he had to believe she was better off with him than a father who cared more about money than his own daughter. He might know nothing about family, but he did know he would never treat her so poorly.

That had to count for something.

After a long silence, she turned to him with a serious gaze that made him tense. "We are here now. We might as well make the best of it."

He arched a brow at her resigned, morose tone. "That's the spirit," he teased.

He was rewarded with another twitch of those lush lips.

One of these days, maybe he'd make her smile.

Did her lover make her smile?

He shoved the thought aside. It wasn't his concern. He didn't need her heart. But if he didn't get inside her body sometime in the very near future, he might go mad.

He shifted now, trying to get comfortable despite the rigid erection between his legs.

"Tell me, Angel, what would you typically do if you were trapped inside on a rainy day at home?"

She looked around them at the bookshelves that lined the room. "Read, I suppose."

"Right. Pretend in this scenario you are stuck inside with a gentleman who's tired of reading and who wishes to be entertained," he said.

She laughed softly. "In this hypothetical situation, are we at the gentleman's home?"

"House," he said. "Not home. I rarely come here, to be honest. I'd thought you'd might want to see it since it's now under your care."

He tried to keep his voice level, but her gaze was far too intent. "You don't enjoy the country?"

He looked away. He liked the country just fine. Just not the silence that came with it. The only times he came here were when he could convince his friends to join him. But more often than not, he was either in town or at one of their estates.

He never did answer, and instead turned it back on her. "We can head back earlier than planned if you'd like. I wouldn't wish for you to be bored—"

"I won't be bored," she said quickly. With a small, tentative smile, she added, "I prefer the country. Always have."

"Ah." His lungs stopped working as his gaze caught on the sweet curve of her lips.

"But if you are not content here—"

"No, no," he said with a dismissive wave. "I can find ways to occupy myself." He couldn't resist flashing her a rakish smile. "I'll admit, most of the activities I'd planned for this trip have been put on hold for the moment."

Her brows drew together in confusion, and then, when he let his gaze roam over her breasts and down to her thighs, he glanced up to see she'd turned pink again.

"Oh," she said.

He chuckled as he adopted his most pompous tone. "This means, of course, that my wife must now find ways to entertain me."

She arched a brow. "Must she?"

"Mmm. She said so in her vows, before God and her family."

Her lips were twitching again, and then an adorable little giggle escaped. "I must have missed that part in the vows."

"Don't worry, Angel." He leaned forward, tapping a finger to his temple. "I remember everything you promised."

"Do you?" She sounded breathless.

Good. That was good. It meant she felt it, too, this stirring of desire that seemed to wrap around them the closer he drew.

"And I remember my promises, as well," he said.

Her eyes flared for a moment, and he knew she was remembering, too. He'd vowed to make her beg.

And by God, he'd see that promise through.

CHAPTER EIGHT

T HE LIBRARY WAS lovely and warm, cozy with its dark wood and overstuffed leather seats.

This was precisely the sort of room Evangeline would have sought out in any country home. The ideal spot to curl up and read while the rain pounded on the panes.

It would have been comfortable indeed—if her companion didn't make her so very uncomfortable.

"How shall we pass the time?" His gaze on her lips said he had ideas.

"Er, reading?" she offered. "I could read aloud if you'd like."

She sounded like a ninny, but it couldn't be helped. After a horrible night of tossing and turning, she'd woken far less emotional and with her mother's voice ringing in her ears. It was time to grow up. Face her life. Make the best of this situation. And here she was, offering to read aloud like he was a child and she, his nurse.

"How about cards?" he said.

She arched her brows. "Cards?"

"Mmm. We can place wagers, make a sport of it."

Her lips parted in surprise. He'd been different today than she'd expected. He hadn't exactly apologized—neither for his highhanded means of getting her to marry him nor for the way he'd driven her to distraction and left her aching and confused last night. But he had been…kind. For him, at least.

He seemed just as determined to find some common ground as she was, and for that, she wanted to meet him halfway. "I, er…I'm afraid I don't know many card games. And I've never wagered on anything before. My mother did not approve of gambling."

His smile faltered a bit, his gaze grew too oddly serious. "No, I should think not."

She frowned. What did that mean?

But then that crooked smile was back, and the creases near his eyes deepened with a genuine smile. "Let me teach you. After all, you're not in your mother's care anymore, are you? You are the mistress of this house. I told you…" He leaned forward. "There are perks to being a duchess."

A surge of something warm, terrifying, and also a little exciting had her holding her breath. He was right. Her parents were not here to disapprove. She was a duchess. And this was her home.

She took a deep, fortifying breath. "Very well. Let us play."

He reached for a deck of cards. "Do you know how to play vingt-un?"

She nodded. "I know the rules. They seem simple enough. But I've never played."

"Then we'll play a few hands to teach you, shall we?" His gaze met hers, and she felt it like a physical force. "And then we shall start to wager."

Her heart seemed to trip over itself in her chest. A warning sounded somewhere in the far reaches of her mind. And yet, she said, "All right."

A few hands later, they agreed she understood well enough to play in earnest.

"If I win," he said, leaning in so close she held her breath. "I will steal a kiss from my wife."

Her lips parted, and her heart tried to lodge itself in her throat. "A-and if I win?"

His smile was slow and made her belly do a flip. "What do you want?"

"I want…" Her brain raced. "I want answers."

He chuckled. "Very well. If you win, you can ask any question you wish, and I shall be obliged to answer you."

She nodded, swallowing hard. She ought to be pleased. Perhaps in this way, she could get to know this man who was such an odd mystery to her. So arrogant one moment, so tender the next. She wasn't entirely sure what to make of him.

She ought to be grateful that she might find out. But she was too nervous to be glad.

He won the first hand, and his grin was nothing short of predatory. He patted his thigh. "Sit on my lap, Angel. I promise I won't bite."

She couldn't draw enough air into her lungs as she did as he asked, perching on the edge of his legs until he laughingly snagged her by the waist and dragged her toward him, so she was cradled in his arms like a child.

Except, she didn't feel like a child. She was painfully aware of her breasts pressing against his chest. Acutely aware of the hard length beneath her bottom, pressing into her thighs.

She let out a puff of air as his stubbled jaw grazed her temple, his breath fanning over her ear. Just like that, the throbbing was back. The ache between her legs had kept her awake all night, and when she'd finally reached down to tentatively explore the sensitive area to see if she could do something to ease her pain, she'd discovered to her horror that she was wet.

And now… *Oh, drat.* She was wet again. And hot. And in pain.

Her breath caught in horror. What was happening to her?

His fingers came beneath her chin and lifted her face to his. "My kiss, Angel." His voice was low, the words a command.

She ought to rebel against that tone, but instead, it made her ache so badly she wiggled to find relief.

He groaned, his lips so close she could feel his heat. "Sit still, love, or I'm going to be demanding far more than kisses."

A pathetic whimper escaped just as his lips closed over hers. This kiss wasn't like last night. It wasn't nearly as tender and gentle. He devoured her mouth with a hungry urgency that should have scared her.

Instead, it made her press into him, her nipples aching to be touched like he'd done the night before, her body surging toward his like it was bereft for the feel of his heat and his touch.

This was insanity. She didn't even like the man; why was she letting him use his tongue like this?

Because he's your husband.

That had her sinking into his arms further. Why fight it? She was his now. This was his right.

That thought made the rest of her qualms up and die without further fight. She opened her lips further, a moan escaping when he slanted his over hers, his tongue claiming her mouth and demanding that she join in.

His tongue stroked hers, teasing and seductive. But his hands never moved from her waist.

Just when she thought she might die from the pleasure of it all, he pulled back and set her on the seat beside him. "Now then," he said as he reached for the cards. "Next round."

He won the next. And then the next.

And each kiss left her trembling like a leaf. It was only kisses, if the word "only" could be applied. Because what he was doing— it was so much more than kissing. He was claiming. He was teaching.

But his hands remained firmly at her waist, and no matter how much she wriggled and pressed against him, he never did do more than kiss her.

Then, at last, she won a round.

He grinned at her when she let out a happy squeal at having finally won.

Leaning back, he eyed her. "What's your question then?"

She had too many, and they were all battling for first place.

But just then, her gaze fell, and her eyes widened at the sight in his pants. She'd felt it beneath her, but seeing it now, jutting up and making his breeches so strained...

Did it ache?

Did it hurt him the way she was hurting? And she did hurt. She had last night, too. And yet, she didn't think that was what her mother had meant or—

His groan cut off her thoughts.

"You're killing me, Angel," he said in a low, gruff voice.

She drew in a sharp breath. Her question. She blurted it out before she could overthink it. "Why do your kisses make me...hurt?"

He blinked, and for a second, she saw sheer fear in his eyes as they fell to her mouth. "Was I too harsh, Angel?" He rubbed his jaw. "Damn. I should have shaved."

"No, no," she said quickly. *Oh drat.* Now her cheeks were so warm she knew without a doubt she must have been beet red. "I didn't mean that."

"Then what—" He stopped short and then grinned. It was a wicked, boyish grin that made her heart beat frantically. But his smug smile disappeared just as quickly as it had appeared as he cleared his throat. "Ah. I believe I know what you mean."

He leaned forward, his hand gently touching her thigh, sliding up until she thought she might scream if he didn't touch her *there.*

But he didn't touch her there. He came close. Agonizingly close. So close that her hips rocked of their own accord as if urging him along, but he didn't go any further.

"Did you hurt last night, Angel? When I left you?" His voice was so gentle.

She nodded.

"I hurt, too," he said.

She turned to face him. "Really?"

"Mmm." He leaned in until his nose touched her temple, his breath covered her ear. "I know how to ease that pain."

She swallowed.

I'll make you beg for it.

Humiliation crept over her, and she dipped her head. Would she beg?

No. No, of course, she wouldn't. Never.

He pulled back as if he could read her thoughts. "But I told you I wouldn't pressure you, Angel, so how about I show you a way that you can ease your pain all by yourself?"

She turned to face him, heedless of her embarrassment. "Is that possible?"

His smile was surprisingly tender, and then he scooped her up like she weighed nothing and settled her back onto his lap, this time with her back to his chest.

"Do you trust me to teach you?" he asked.

Her pulse beat loudly in her ears. The moment felt weighted. *Do you trust me?* She wet her lips, her breasts straining against her gown. *Did* she trust him?

"You're my husband," she said softly.

It wasn't really an answer, and his gruff, humorless laugh said he knew as much.

"That's right, Angel." His low voice was so close to her ear, it made her shiver. "I'm your husband. The only man who will ever touch you here." His hand came up to cup her breast.

She gasped and arched, but his hand dropped just as quickly to clutch the fabric of her skirts.

"And I am most certainly the only man on God's green earth who will ever have the pleasure of touching you here."

She held her breath as his hands roughly snatched up her skirts. Embarrassment and curiosity and that aching, needy pain were sudden and overwhelming. She squeezed her eyes shut, dropping her head back against his shoulder as he brought her skirts all the way up and then made short work of divesting her of her undergarments.

The feel of air on that wet heat between her thighs had her breath growing labored.

"Open your eyes, Angel." It was a gruff, harsh command again, and she didn't dare to disobey.

Her eyes opened, and she looked down, humiliated and oddly aroused even more by the sight of her own bare thighs. Soft curls covered her *mons*, but she'd never really looked at herself down there, and the fact that he was seeing this, too…

"I'm too embarrassed," she whispered.

"You are the most beautiful sight I've ever beheld." It was the awe and reverence in his voice as he looked down at her from over her shoulder that had her swallowing down her embarrassment.

She was his, after all. This was his right.

He kissed her temple and then her ear. "I won't hurt you, love. I won't even touch you."

She blinked, dismayed a bit by this new fact. "Y-you won't?"

"I told you, tonight, you are learning how to ease your own ache."

She whimpered, not sure herself if she was protesting or urging him to get on with it. A fire had formed in her belly, and it was flickering down into her womb.

"I told you, Angel. When I take you as a man takes a woman, it will be because you beg me for it." He nipped the lobe of her ear, making her gasp. "Are you ready to beg me to take you, Angel?"

She paused, panting for air. And then she gave a sharp shake of her head, a surge of anger taking hold at his arrogance and his games.

He wanted all of her. She understood that now. He wanted to break her. Tame her. Make her his biddable bride.

She clung to thoughts of Albert. That was who she loved. A man who was kind and gentle, who cared for her in a way that made her feel understood. He'd never pressured her to speak. He'd never so much as stolen a kiss.

He'd certainly never insisted she beg.

This dratted man. She shouldn't be enjoying his touch. It was a betrayal to Albert, wasn't it?

But then again, they'd both known that marriage would mean she'd be intimate with another.

His loud exhale beside her ear made her start.

"Fair enough," he said. "You're still not ready."

Her body slumped back. She hadn't even realized she'd been tensed to flee, but now she sagged into him, knowing that he'd dropped the question. For now, at least, she did not have to sort out her feelings about Albert and this new intimacy with her husband.

"You're a romantic, Angel," the duke said as his hands started to stroke her thighs, slowly, leisurely, like they had all the time in the world.

"Is that so bad?" Her voice was too breathless.

This was torture. The area between her thighs throbbed as his fingers strummed over her thighs, down the outside and then up over the top, dipping down to the seam where she pressed her knees together.

If she hadn't felt his manhood stabbing into her lower back, she might have thought he was utterly unaffected.

"It's not a bad trait, I suppose," he said like they were having a philosophical chat over a leisurely meal. "Romance is fine when it comes to novels and operas. But in real life, you ought to know that there's no connection between the heart and the body, nor the mind, for that matter."

Her chest prickled with unease at his aloof tone and the cold words. All so very unemotional, though he touched her with such tender intimacy.

"What does that mean?" She could barely speak as he gently slid his fingers between her legs and nudged her knees apart.

"It means you can enjoy the pleasures of the flesh without betraying the one in your heart."

She squeezed her eyes shut. That didn't seem right. It sounded like justifications and excuses. But then, he had her legs parted, and in one move, he slid his knees up between hers and used them to wedge her thighs apart.

"Oh!" She didn't fight him, but her lungs labored for air. She was spread wide, her feminine folds parted, revealing her soft, wet opening.

Her lips parted with shock at the indecent sight, a mix of horror, humiliation, and hot liquid heat sending her mind reeling and her heart racing.

"Beautiful," he groaned, his head falling against the crook of her neck as his fingers clutched her inner thighs. His teeth gently nipped at the spot where her neck met her shoulder, and she shivered at the unexpected thrill it sent through her. Her nipples puckered.

Beautiful. The word cut through her horror. There was no mockery in his tone, only sincerity. Perhaps even reverence.

"Am I beautiful?" she whispered, embarrassment tightening her throat.

"You have no idea, Angel." He groaned into her hair. "You cannot imagine what the sight of your wet, tight quim does to me." His hips jerked up roughly as he spoke, that hard shaft rubbing against her bottom.

She was panting for air now. His words were so crass. What they were doing was wrong. It had to be.

But then again, he was her husband. This was his right. Surely he knew what he was doing.

She wiggled her hips tentatively against him and was flooded with satisfaction when he moaned, his hands coming up to cup her breasts in a move that spoke of desperation.

Gone were the cool words and practical tone as he kneaded her flesh through her tight bodice. "Christ, Angel, you feel like heaven."

A huff of shock escaped at the urgency in his tone as well as the sacrilege words.

But his lewd thoughts and the sight of her bare sex were no longer evoking horror, nor even disgust. Not the way they ought. She wasn't sure what it was she was feeling, but it was overwhelming. Intoxicating.

"W-what are you doing?" she stammered, her whole body tensing as his hands began to move again. She tried to clench her thighs shut, but his legs kept them apart.

She was at his mercy. A fact that ought to scare her. Instead, she found herself sinking back into his embrace.

"There's nothing to be ashamed of, Angel," he said, his voice so very gruff and heartachingly earnest. "This is your body, and it is perfection."

"Is it?" Her voice was too high and weak. She barely recognized it.

"It's perfection," he said again, his tone brooking no arguments. "And it's mine."

The harshness in his voice made her shudder, and her hips jerked.

"That's it," he whispered against her skin, watching alongside her as that patch of curls grew soaking wet. "You want it, love. Your body needs it."

Her head rolled from side to side. "Help me," she whimpered.

He muttered a curse before grabbing one of her hands with his and lacing his fingers over hers. "I've got you, Angel," he muttered. And then he slid both their hands between her thighs, covering her mound and making her jerk upright with shock at the new sensation of his fingers down there.

Of *her* fingers down there.

He held them still, cupping her wetness as she gasped and panted. Her upper back was arching now as her breasts begged for attention.

She was needy. Everywhere.

"Easy, pet," he said, his tongue flicking her ear. "This is only the start. Remember that. When you're ready to ask like a good little girl, I'll make this bliss seem like nothing."

"This bliss?" She repeated the word in disbelief. This wasn't bliss. It was torture.

His low chuckle slid over her like a caress as his fingers moved over hers, guiding her in an exploration of the hot, wet folds.

"See how silky and smooth you are," he crooned softly, his low words of praise soothing her embarrassment. "So beautiful, Angel."

"It hurts," she whispered as he guided one of her fingers into her own slick channel. She cried out at the new sensation.

"It's a good sort of pain, Angel. Embrace it."

When she pulled her finger out, terrified by her own naughty deeds, he kissed her temple and took hold of her fingers once more, sliding them up and down, up and down, exploring her entrance, and then—

"Raff!" She shouted his name when he brought her fingers over her hard, tight nub.

His knees pushed outward, spreading her as far as she could go. His hips rolled up, and his hardness ground into her.

He removed his hands from hers to clutch her hips. "Touch yourself," he commanded. "Rub that spot, and don't stop until you find that bliss."

His voice was grating, commanding. So harsh, she knew she ought to protest. "I need your help," she whispered instead. Embarrassment held her captive, and she froze in place without his hand over hers helping her, guiding her.

Now it was just her, and she felt...dirty. This was not how a proper young lady behaved. Not even after her wedding.

He grunted, the sound pained like he was the one being tortured and not her. "I told you I would show you how to ease your own pain."

She whimpered, the ache so intense she choked on a sob.

"Would it make you feel better if I find my own relief as well?" he asked.

She could hear the smirk in his voice, and it made her hips arch again. "Yes."

He gripped her hips hard. "I'm going to use you, pet. I'm

going to dirty this pretty gown of yours."

"I don't care," she moaned.

He used his grip on her hips to slide her to one leg, and then he freed his erection. She barely got a good look before glancing away, but it was enough to know that he was long and thick and…oh sweet heavens. "How is that supposed to fit?"

He chuckled. "That's a problem for another day." He turned her head and kissed her, thrusting his tongue into her mouth as he gripped her hand and brought it back to that sensitive nub.

"Make your master proud," he said harshly against her lips. "Show me how you like to be touched."

She didn't need any more encouragement because her fingers had already found that magical spot and the sight of him taking himself in hand…

She gasped at the sight, so unusual and so erotic as he stroked himself over and over, his gaze fixed on her fingers between her thighs, all the while.

"That's right, Angel," he praised her again and again. "Stroke yourself until you come. Show me how wet you are. Show me how much you want to be bedded, my naughty girl."

She barely understood his vulgar words, but they did something to her—they made her feel wild and uncontrollable.

They made her feel something more than that.

As her head fell back with a moan and every muscle inside her began to tense in anticipation, the word came to her.

Power.

She felt powerful.

His grunts and groans and his murmurs about her beauty grew more and more frantic. He was driven just as mad as she was, and that knowledge made her forget the last of her embarrassment.

"You're going to make me come so hard," he said, his normally smug smile nowhere to be found as he gritted his teeth and stroked himself hard.

"I—I—" She didn't know how to tell him what was happening, but he seemed to know.

With his free hand, he reached around and slid a hand into her bodice, cupping one of her breasts. His fingers found her taut nipple and pinched it hard.

She cried out, and with one more frantic rub between her thighs, she screamed as her body came apart.

The throbbing tension gave way to an explosion of sensations that left her trembling in its wake.

A second later, her husband groaned into her ear as he found his own release.

For a moment, they stayed just as they were, panting. As reality set back in, she closed her trembling legs and tugged down her skirts. Her sluggish mind was trying to work, trying to sort out how she should be feeling.

Truthfully, she couldn't feel much more than spent. Exhausted and…relieved.

"Now then," Raff said, that crooked, smug smile back in place as he cleaned himself up and straightened his own clothes. "What do you say we play another round?"

CHAPTER NINE

HIS ANGEL WAS avoiding him.

Raff knew it, and he couldn't say he blamed her. She'd hurried up to her own rooms the night before after their card games...and other activities. She'd been nowhere to be found all day today.

Well, that wasn't entirely true. He'd heard from his servants that she'd asked to explore the grounds.

Why she hadn't asked him, he preferred not to know. It was humiliating enough that his new wife hadn't actually wanted to become his wife. The fact that he wasn't currently in her bed and buried inside her was even more insulting.

And yet, it was the fact that she'd opted to tour his grounds on her own that gnawed at him today. He glanced out the window at the overcast day.

Perhaps that was because he was rather bored himself. This was precisely why he rarely came to this house and never alone. There were too many memories here.

Not bad ones. Not good ones either. Just empty ones. Lonely ones.

Wasn't a wife supposed to make a place feel less lonely?

"Lady Raffian has returned, Your Grace," the butler announced from the doorway of his study.

"Good. Very good. Will you ask Her Grace if she would be

kind enough to join me for dinner this evening."

"Yes, Your Grace."

Raff stared out the window some more, wondering how his life had come to this. How *he*, the Duke of Raffian, was all but begging his bride to share a meal with him.

He let out a humorless huff of laughter as he imagined what his friends would say.

Oh, how the mighty have fallen.

But when Evangeline joined him later that evening, he had no regrets about asking her to join him. She was dazzling in a shimmering blue gown that made her eyes sparkle and her skin glow. Her hair was half down, and the long locks shone, begging to be touched.

She begged to be touched.

And now that he'd watched her bring herself satisfaction, he wasn't sure how much longer he could survive without touching her. Their interlude had been erotic and revealing.

And torture, plain and simple.

"My lady," he murmured as he held out her seat for her himself, sending the other servants out of the room the moment the plates were laden with food.

"Did you enjoy your time exploring the grounds today?" he asked.

"I did, Your—Raff."

He chuckled at her near slip, and when she peeked over with an impish grin, he could hardly swallow his wine for the sudden knot in his throat.

Good God. How the mighty have fallen, indeed.

He drew in a deep breath. It was lust, of course. It had been from the start. The sooner he made her acknowledge the attraction between them, the sooner he could fuck her right out of his system.

Even the most alluring woman lost some of her shine once the novelty wore off. And his wife would be no different.

"Tell me what you saw," he said. Her sudden, answering

smile gave him pause. "What's so amusing?"

"It is your property, Raff. I'm certain you already know what I saw and who I met."

He arched a brow, ignoring the first part. "You met people during your outing?"

"Mmm," she said as she took a sip of soup. "I met quite a few people on my walk into town."

"You...walked into town?" He sounded like a fool repeating her words back to her, but it couldn't be helped. He'd thought she'd merely wandered the gardens or perhaps trekked through the surrounding meadows.

"Yes. I brought Mrs. Harper with me as a chaperone." She paused with her spoon still raised. "You do not mind, do you?"

"No. No, of course not, I just..." He cleared his throat. "I should have liked to have shown you the local sights myself."

"Oh." Her cheeks turned a delicate shade of pink. "I apologize. I thought you would be busy. My father spends most of his time working when we're at our country house, so I just assumed..."

Working on what? Raff wanted to ask. The man had clearly convinced his daughter he was a well-to-do, responsible landowner, but Tracker's findings had made it clear just what a wastrel he was. The mother, too, if her excessive spending were anything to go by.

And all without a thought for their daughter's future.

He was split right down the middle between guilt and pride as she smiled at him shyly now.

Her future was in his hands. She was his responsibility.

He'd had nothing but responsibilities on his plate since he was a child, but none had ever felt quite so momentous as this. For a moment, his confidence was shaken. "I would not hurt you, Angel."

She blinked in surprise at his sudden outburst, and he cleared his throat.

Bloody hell, he sounded like a lunatic. "What I meant to say," he continued, "was that I know we've had a rather unusual start, you and I. But I hope you know that you can trust me."

To his surprise, she turned a brighter shade of red. "Do you mean…" She visibly swallowed. "Are you referring to last night?"

If she ducked her head any further, she'd be face first in her soup bowl.

"No, actually," he said, unable to hide the amusement in his voice. "I'd hope that by now you realize I would not harm you physically. I merely meant that when it comes to your future and your happiness, I take my responsibility for your care very seriously."

She lifted her head slowly. "Thank you. I appreciate you saying so."

A silence fell, and it grew too heavy. Raff took a sip of his drink. Who was this man sitting in his chair? Making solemn vows over soup and fretting over a lady's happiness? He hardly recognized himself.

Moreover, he'd stopped himself from taking her twice now. *Twice.*

He was either losing his faculties or had grown addled without a woman's body under his. He hadn't tupped anyone since he'd seen Evangeline all those weeks ago, and that, for him, was something of a miracle.

"What else did you do while you were out?" he asked.

She brightened. "I explored the gardens. Even though they're not in bloom yet, they truly are a wonder."

"Mmm," he agreed. Were they? He supposed his gardener was due an increase in wages.

She leaned forward. "Do you visit the gardens often?"

"No," he said. "I'm rarely in residence here, if you'll recall."

"Ah yes," she sank back in her seat as if disappointed. Her words from the night before came back to him. She preferred the country, hadn't she said that?

"You could make a home for yourself here," he offered. The moment he said it, he felt as though he'd stepped in horse dung.

Her look of dismay was slight, but he caught it.

He shifted in his seat. "That is, I thought you liked it here."

"Yes, I do," she said quickly. "I just wondered…did you mean…that is…" She sighed and then dropped her spoon onto her plate. "I apologize, Raff. I am not very good with this sort of thing."

"What sort of thing is that?" he asked, torn between amusement and dread at her sudden candor.

"The talking sort of thing," she said with a wince.

"Again, I must beg to differ," he said. "You were very clear the other night when you told me how you felt about me."

He was teasing, but she blushed again. "Yes, well, I was angry then."

"I see." He set his spoon down as well. "Would it help you to speak your mind if I made you angry again?"

Her lips twitched with mirth.

He held his hands out and feigned innocence. "I am here to help you in any way I can. Shall I insult your precious books? Your mother, perhaps? I am afraid I cannot insult your looks because not even I am that good of a liar."

She dropped her head with another blush, but he caught her smile. "You are teasing me."

"I am." He leaned forward. "But I will tell you this, Evangeline. As much as I did not enjoy hearing about your infatuation with another nor your distaste for me, I did very much appreciate your honesty."

Her gaze lifted to meet his. "You did?"

"I did." He paused. He didn't actually mean to say anymore, but her bright, curious gaze seemed to urge him on. "I inherited the dukedom at a young age, you know—"

"Yes, I'd heard," she murmured.

"Aside from a few close friends from my school days—friends who are brutally honest with me, I'm afraid to say—I've grown accustomed to being surrounded by simpering sycophants. The fact that you are not, pleases me."

Her eyes widened slightly, and her lips parted.

He sat back, suddenly uncomfortable at the way she was watching him. He'd shared too much. Waving a hand, his voice grew brisque. "So, get on with it. What did you wish to say?"

She cleared her throat and looked down at hands before taking a deep breath and lifting her gaze to meet his once more. "Your comment made me wonder about what you foresee for me. What you…expect of me."

His lips curved up as his gaze caught on her lips. "As my wife, you mean?"

He'd rather thought that much was obvious.

"Yes, I mean after…Er, after…"

"After I get you with child?" he offered. He couldn't quite hide his amusement at her embarrassment.

Had she forgotten that he'd touched her intimately the night before? How many times and in how many ways would he have to touch her before she lost that sweet shyness that had her blushing so often?

He aimed to find out.

"Yes," she said. Straightening, she kept her focus on the candles that were situated in the center of the table. "As I said yesterday, I do enjoy the country more than the city. Once I have your children, I could stay here?"

"Yes." His answer was too short. Hadn't he said as much the other day?

She toyed with her spoon. "And you would…you would stay elsewhere?"

His jaw worked. "Yes."

All his amusement faded fast. So that was what she'd been wondering. How quickly and easily she could get him out of her life. Planning on having a nice, cozy family life here in the country on her own, was she?

Silence fell again, and this time, he found no need to end it. It had been idiotic to think a dinner together might change anything. Besides, what did he care if she wanted his company or not? All that mattered was getting between those legs.

His gaze lifted, and he found her watching him before she dropped her own gaze down to her meal.

He might have his faults, but he wasn't about to be cuckolded, and he sure as hell wasn't going to be kept out of his wife's bed.

That's what he ought to be focused on. Making her ache so badly that she dropped down onto her knees and begged him to bed her.

He set his glass down with a clink so loud she jumped.

All in good time, he told himself.

All in good time.

CHAPTER TEN

EVANGELINE TOYED WITH the embroidery on her blanket as she stared up at her bedroom ceiling.

Raff had been true to his word. That first night she'd waited for him to return to her bedroom, tossing and turning, certain he would come back to claim what was his.

But he hadn't.

And it was becoming abundantly clear that he would honor his word. He would wait for her to come to him. To *beg* him.

She scowled at the ceiling. Impossible man.

And yet…

There was that sensation again, coiling in her belly and refusing to let her sleep. It was restlessness, yes, as she couldn't quite settle. But it was more than that. It was heavy and nagging and…

Guilt.

It was guilt. She flipped onto her side and squeezed her eyes shut, but that did no good. If anything, it made this twisting, slithering sensation worsen because all she could see was the look on Raff's face this evening when she'd asked about her future.

He'd shut down. That was the only way she could think to describe it.

He'd shut her out.

For a little while, dining with him had almost been…cozy. Talking to him had been surprisingly easy. He'd worn a smile, yes, but it hadn't been taunting. It hadn't been patronizing either. He'd listened to her with what seemed to be genuine interest. His gaze had fixed on her, and he'd… Well, he'd *listened*.

Listening oughtn't be such an enormous act, but in her experience, listening was not a common occurrence. She was a young lady. Her role was to be seen, not heard. How often had she been told that as a child?

Her father had no patience for her talking, and not even her mother had taken much interest in her hobbies or pastimes. And so, she'd learned to keep her mouth shut. But for a little while at dinner, she'd felt as though he'd actually wanted her to speak. And in turn, he'd been…different.

Not necessarily open. But not nearly so aloof as she'd expected. She'd gotten a glimpse past his walls. And she realized…that was what it was. His mockery, his laughter. His smug arrogance. It was a defense. All part of the ducal facade one might expect.

At least, she thought perhaps it might be.

She flopped onto her other side and plumped her pillow with a bit too much force.

Oh drat. She wasn't used to being plagued by guilt, and she did not care for it. She tried to steer her thoughts to her day in town. A day spent watching townsfolk and shopkeepers stare, whispers following in her wake.

From what she could gather, the Duke of Raffian was not exactly beloved by the people. The amount of awe and reverence that followed in her wake made her feel quite set apart.

Was that how Raff felt? She did not think he was lying when he'd said he was typically surrounded by sycophants.

And when she'd joined him for dinner, there was a moment when he'd looked so lonely.

She flopped onto her back once more.

Loneliness. That was the emotion she'd seen when she'd joined him at dinner. Wasn't it? She could have sworn he'd been relieved to have her company. And when she'd spoken bluntly…

Her stomach formed a knot.

Again with the guilt. And the sympathy. After all, loneliness was something she could well understand. And the guilt? Well, that had nothing to do with his conversation and everything to do with the look he'd given her when she'd asked about the future.

Had she hurt his feelings?

She frowned up at the ceiling. Impossible.

He'd only married her to have his way with her in bed.

Instantly her cheeks grew warm, and her pulse grew fluttery. Though, for a man who'd only wanted her for her beauty and to have her in his bed… He hadn't yet claimed her in that way, now had he?

She sighed harshly as she sat up. Oh, this was useless. She couldn't stay here fretting all night.

She threw back the covers with a sigh.

She wouldn't bother the servants this late at night, but a warm cup of milk would do the trick. Her night rail cinched tight, Evangeline padded through the great house and to the kitchen.

Once there, she let out a cry of alarm. Her squeak was perhaps a bit unwarranted. Raff had hardly snuck up on her. If anything, one might argue that *she* had snuck up on *him*. He had a candle on the counter and was helping himself to a slice of bread. He arched a brow as she hovered in the doorway. "Trouble sleeping?"

She nodded.

His gaze dropped, sweeping over her and seeming to see everything despite the dim light. "Hungry, were you?"

His voice was so low that the seemingly innocent somehow managed to seem indecent.

She pressed her legs together as that now familiar, yet still strange sensation made her lower belly feel heavy and her limbs shake. "I was just going to fetch some milk."

"Allow me," he said.

Surely he was joking. But then, in three short strides, he was standing just in front of her, and he lifted her at her waist like she weighed nothing before setting her on the countertop beside the candle. "Your bare feet will get cold on the stone floor," he said.

As if that was an explanation.

As if he actually cared about her feet.

She pressed her lips together, nerves making her heart race as she watched him. Why she was nervous, she couldn't quite say.

It was a sensation she could not shake around him. It was as if the very air around him quivered in expectation.

Maybe that was what came with being a powerful man who ruled over so many. His actions could affect so many. Why, he could ruin lives with the sweep of his signature.

Wasn't that what he'd done to her?

Ruined her life? She frowned. That seemed too harsh even in her thoughts. He'd destroyed her plans for her life. Her dreams. Not her life.

She bit her lip as she watched him work.

It felt wrong to think about Albert here and now while in this man's house. In *her* house.

An odd sound escaped. Heavens, she was still trying to come to grips with all that had changed.

He looked over with a curious expression. "All right?" he asked.

She nodded. "I just...I still feel a bit odd, I suppose."

He stilled, a jug of milk in his hands. "How so?"

She was grateful he couldn't see her flaming cheeks as she watched him. With only his shirt on, and open at the collar...it was impossible not to notice the muscles on his back and arms. The flickering candlelight seemed to call attention with his every move.

"Angel?" His low voice cut into her wandering thoughts.

"Oh, I just...I only meant..." She swallowed hard. "Being in a new home. Being someone's wife—" *Being the wrong person's wife.* "I suppose it takes some getting used to, that's all."

"Several weeks was not enough?" The question sounded mild, but she felt just as she did at the dinner table.

As though she'd offended him. Which was silly.

"I did not believe this would actually transpire," she admitted. "Not at first. Not for a while. I thought my father would see reason, you see."

He didn't say a word. Not one. His silence made her tense. When at last he brought her milk, perfectly warmed, and settled it into her hands, her whole body was quivering beneath the heavy silence.

"I did not mean to offend," she whispered.

His gaze met hers, darker than ever in the candlelight. "Nonsense. You did not offend. You merely spoke the truth, and I told you earlier that I appreciate honesty." One side of his mouth hitched up. "Even if it is not particularly pleasant."

She mashed her lips together to keep from apologizing again. Why was she apologizing? She'd never wanted this marriage, and he was the one who'd forced her hand.

Her brows drew together as she remembered what he'd said. He hadn't believed her father. Wasn't that what he'd said the other night?

Her father had said she did not wish to marry him, and he had not believed him. But why?

Her stomach sank low as she tried to imagine the conversation between her father and her husband.

Was it Raff who'd forced her hand? Or her father? That knot in her belly seemed to tumble and turn in a sickening manner.

"Now, now, child," he said, gently smoothing a thumb between her brows to ease her frown of confusion. "No need to fret so."

Her frown only intensified. "I'm not a child."

The words seemed to echo harshly because of her tone? It had sounded…childish. And the way she was seated, in her night rail and with her feet dangling?

She hardly felt like an elegant lady.

And then there was the fact that she was clutching warm milk.

"Drat," she muttered.

His smile was slow, and it made her belly flip. "You are not a child," he agreed.

But she *had* been childish. She swallowed hard at the self-accusatory thought. It wasn't her mother's words coming back to haunt her, and it wasn't Raff saying it.

Worse, she had the nagging suspicion that she'd been standing on the wrong foot all the while. Angry at the wrong man. Fighting him in all the wrong ways.

Her breath caught as her mind called up an image of his hand over hers, buried between her thighs.

"I…I'm sorry," she mumbled. "I just don't like to be called a child."

"You don't like when I call you child, nor Angel, nor Angie," he said. "I'm at a loss as to what to call you, I'm afraid."

"Angel," she said. It came out on a whisper that had his brows hitching up. She lifted a shoulder. "I've grown used to it."

His smile grew. "Very well, then…Angel. Is that what has you up tonight, unable to sleep?" He leaned in, and all she could smell was his scent. Liquor and spice and soap. It was heady and…pleasant. Almost homey.

She didn't answer immediately, and then she couldn't answer at all as his hands came to rest on either side of her thighs. Her breath caught in her throat. She was effectively trapped, with him standing so close her knees brushed his ribcage, and his face was even with hers.

"Pardon?" she said.

He reached out and touched the lower lip she'd been worrying, making her gasp as a jolt of sensation shot through her at the intimate touch.

"Are you up fretting over your lost love?"

His voice was taunting, but his eyes…

Oh, his eyes made that guilt twist and writhe. There was no anger, but she was nearly certain she caught a flicker of hurt.

"No," she admitted.

And then her guilt reared up again, but this time toward Albert. She *hadn't* been thinking of him. Not one of her many conflicted thoughts had been about the man she'd forsaken.

So no, she hadn't been thinking of Albert. But perhaps she should have been.

"Did you and this gentleman have an understanding?" he asked as she took a sip of milk.

She shook her head. "Not officially. But he spoke to me about possibly one day…"

She trailed off as Raff's eyes darkened. "He spoke to you without speaking to your father first? Well…" His voice lightened with mockery. "Perhaps I did not give this rogue credit. Nor you, it would seem."

She stiffened. "It wasn't like that. He took no liberties. And he did speak to my father. That is, he would have spoken to him again, and—"

"I see."

She set her cup down, her spine straightening at his taunting tone. He did not see. "He asked my father for permission to court me, and my father insisted that I have a Season first and—"

"Yes, yes. And then the wicked duke came along and stole you away," he finished, his tone dry but his eyes flashing dangerously.

"Something like that," she murmured.

"And your father knew your feelings on the matter," he continued.

Something about the way he was talking made her feel like he was prying. He phrased it as a statement, but there was a question implicit there as well. Almost as if he wasn't certain what he knew.

Or what *she* knew.

She frowned at the thought that he knew more about her father's mind than she did.

"My father knew my opinion," she said slowly. "But he thought that my feelings were childish."

The word hung heavy again.

"I believe my father thought I would no longer wish to marry him once I'd met other gentlemen of higher rank and with greater wealth."

"Ah, so this man is not so very rich and powerful," he said.

"No." She huffed. "And I did not care."

"But your father did."

She didn't answer. The answer was clear.

"Were you in love with this man for long?" His careless tone made her stiffen. But when she went to shift away, his hands caught her thighs, and that place low in her belly gave a tug that left her breathless.

"Not long," she said. "His family took over the estate near ours two years ago, and over time, we became friends."

She pursed her lips because…that did not sound right. Albert wasn't her friend. He was too handsome for that. It had taken her a year just to speak to him in anything other than blushes and stammers. It was only the past months leading up to her engagement that he'd begun to express his ardor. And always so sweetly. A stolen touch of her hand. A poem slipped into her book. All of the romantic gestures that she'd read about as a girl.

She blushed as she ducked her head. No doubt Raff would laugh at such things. He'd think them childish, for certain. And she didn't want to give him any more reasons to doubt her maturity.

His fingers caught her chin and gently lifted her head, so she was forced to meet his gaze, her lips parting.

"I'm sorry," he said.

He dropped his hand, but her lips remained parted. He was apologizing? What for?

His lips twitched as though her shock amused him. "I may not say it often, but I am capable of regret, you know."

"And do you regret marrying me?" Her insides stilled. She felt as though her very existence rested on his answer.

He scoffed. "Christ, no."

Her brows drew together in confusion.

"I'm sorry that you were hurt. I regret that I didn't give you the time and attention that you deserved from a courtship." He leaned in close until his lips were so close, she could feel his breath on her cheek. "But I'll never apologize for taking what's mine."

She swallowed hard, her heart scrambling in her chest like it was trying to get out. "I wasn't yours when you claimed me."

I'll never be yours. That was what she ought to have said. *You'll never have my heart.*

Wasn't that what she'd said their first night together?

She still meant it.

Didn't she?

He dropped a light kiss on the edge of her lips. "You don't like being claimed, Angel, is that it? You don't wish to be mine?"

There was that teasing again—that taunting. But combined with the way he feathered kisses over her jaw, her cheeks…close to her mouth but not actually kissing her the way she wanted.

Oh, dear. She did want him to kiss her.

She sat back in alarm.

"That's all right, Angel," he continued, catching her by the back of her neck to hold her still. "That's why I'm waiting for you to claim me."

Her throat worked, but no words would come. Not a protest. Not even a "no."

"Is that why you came down here, love?" he continued, his voice wrapping around her and making her limbs grow heavy. "Were you seeking me out to beg, Angel?"

"W-what? N-no, of course not." A flare of wicked heat between her thighs begged to differ.

She *hadn't* been seeking him out. Had she?

She'd merely wanted milk.

His hands splayed over her thighs, his thumbs settling on the inside and digging into her soft flesh, but he didn't part her legs again. He held still. "Tell me what you want."

Her eyes widened. What did she want? She didn't know where to start.

What mattered now was how they moved forward.

"What?" He kissed her nose. "Do." He kissed her chin. "You." He kissed her forehead. "Want?" He grazed the lightest kiss over her lips. So light, she could barely feel it.

She leaned in as he pulled away.

She just barely bit back a growl of frustration.

Why? Why did he keep doing that? One moment he seemed to her a…a *man*. A man, not just a duke. More than a title. And then he'd do this. Pull away, whether by shutting her out with coldness or physically to deny her pleasure.

It was maddening.

What did she want?

She wanted the same thing she'd wanted the day before when they'd gambled on cards.

She wanted answers.

Her hands came to his shirt, and she clenched the material, making his eyes flare slightly in surprise. "Why is this place not your home?"

It was a silly question, but it was a start.

He shrugged. "I prefer London."

"And why are you surrounded by sycophants?"

He smirked. "Because I am a duke."

She frowned. This wasn't what she wanted at all. She wanted answers. She wanted truth. She wanted…more. She wanted to see the man behind the title. To know for certain what lay beneath all the taunting and the swagger.

When she glanced back up, she saw his gaze had settled on her lips. Her head seemed to spin as her lungs struggled for air.

"Why are you down here in the kitchen tonight?" she asked, her voice a whisper as he leaned in so close his chest brushed against her breasts.

"I couldn't sleep," he said.

"Me neither."

"Were you hungry, Angel?" he asked.

She nodded.

His grin was sudden and wicked. "So was I."

"W-what are you doing?" Her voice rose sharply as he swept aside the contents of the countertop behind her in one quick move.

"Lean back, Angel," he said.

"Why?"

He laughed. "Because I believe you are just as hungry as I am. Just as restless." His gaze dropped down between her thighs, and she felt an ache so intense it made her whimper.

He tsked. "Poor little darling. I thought so. I have no doubt that if I were to touch you there, you'd be so very wet for me."

Her cheeks were on fire. Why was she wet? Was that normal? Her mother never said anything about that. Part of her wanted to ask, but humiliation stopped her.

He thrust her legs apart, and she squeaked—to her horror, but the sound wasn't a protest.

To her great regret, she wasn't even afraid.

To her everlasting shame, she was…excited. Breathless to see what he'd do next.

"One of us ought to find relief," he murmured. His hands were already hitching up her skirts. "Let me see your breasts, Angel."

"W-what?"

He speared her with a look that made her hot and cold at once. There was a command in his eyes that she could not deny. Nerves and excitement thrummed through her as she unknotted her nightrail and pulled it open, her fingers working the buttons down the front of her gown.

"That's it," he said. "You'll be begging me soon enough, Angel. Once you see how good it can be."

She wanted to argue, but the place between her thighs was throbbing, and she shifted restlessly as she willed him to touch her. But he wouldn't. Not without something in return.

She slid the gown from her shoulders and held her breath as her skin was revealed.

"Bloody hell," he muttered. His eyes flashed hot and dangerous, a muscle clenching tight in his jaw.

She might have thought him angry if that heat in his eyes wasn't so very hungry.

She glanced down, embarrassed but not frightened at the sight of his hard length stretching against his breeches.

His hands came to her breasts gently. Almost lovingly, he seemed to weigh them in his palms. "So beautiful." He flicked his thumbs over the already taut nipples, and she whimpered, her hips jerking.

That made him smile. He looked like a wolf as his gaze met hers, hungry and fierce. "Do you like that, love?" He pinched her nipples harder, and she gasped as her hips rocked.

"I don't know what you're doing to me," she said.

His gaze softened, his touch, too.

She shivered as his fingers caressed the swell of her breasts, over the tips, and around the sides.

"I told you, Angel. I'm showing you that you have nothing to fear with me. You don't have to love me to find satisfaction. And I think we'll both enjoy this marriage far more if we learn to find our pleasures where we can."

The words hit wrong. Ever since she'd arrived in this kitchen, she'd been feeling like a target with arrows piercing her in all the soft spots, but that last comment made her stomach drop and her heart clench.

Find our pleasures where we can.

So practical. So…wrong. So not what she wanted from marriage. No talk of love, of family, of—

She gasped as his hands dropped back down to shove her thighs apart roughly, the skirts all the way up now to reveal her bare core.

"I told you I was hungry," he said with a devilish smile. And then he did the unthinkable.

He buried his head between her thighs, and he kissed her *there*. His mouth covered her sex, open and hot. His tongue pressed between her folds in a wide, penetrating lick before he pulled back and gentled his touch.

Her cry of shock turned into a wail as sensations raced through her, too overwhelming to know if they were good or bad, pain or pleasure.

Her head fell back as he nuzzled her folds, his lips tender and firm just like when he kissed her mouth, and the stubble on his jaw scraping her inner thighs.

Pleasure. Her head fell back as his tongue flicked out to trace along the slit of her seam.

Definitely pleasure.

His tongue was teasing and coy, flicking out softly and then harder as he explored her womanhood, from her tight channel all the way up to that hard little nub.

Her hips rocked as he spread her wider, his hands moving to cup her bottom, so he was lifting her up.

This was so wrong. So very wrong.

"Oh, oh...." It was all she could say as her hips jerked and rocked, pleasure making her tilt her hips up even further to meet his mouth and embarrassment making her wiggle away.

She was in a blasted wrestling match with herself. "I can't, I can't," she said.

He growled against her heat before lifting his head to meet her gaze. "You can," he said before licking her once more with one long stroke all the way from her bottom to that sensitive nub. "You can, and I will."

She shivered at the harshness in his voice. The firm command that made her feel at once helpless and at ease.

She had no choice in the matter. There was no debate. She was his, after all.

He didn't let her argue any more after that, burying his face and laying siege to her womanhood. His tongue licked her wide and soft before he hardened it to a point to tease her fleshy folds.

She was all out writhing now, lying flat on the counter with her hands buried in his hair.

She told herself she was trying to stop him, but her nails dug into his scalp as she held him closer, grinding herself against his hot mouth for more.

"More." The plea slipped out of her, and she felt his firm, wicked lips curve up in a smile between her thighs.

When his tongue teased her entrance, she moaned.

She was still achy and empty even as her limbs trembled from the onslaught of sensation.

"This is where I'll take you, Angel," he growled, his hands releasing his grip on her buttocks to slide a thick finger into her channel. "This is where I'll bury my cock inside of you and pound into you until you come so hard you scream bloody murder."

She gasped, whimpers escaping as he drove that finger deep inside of her over and over again.

"So wet," he groaned.

His words should have horrified her, but all she could do was lift her head to watch as he worked some magic that had a tight cord building between her womb and her breasts.

She needed him to touch her breasts again. Her skin was raw, her nipples so tight. With a moan, she arched her breasts high, and then...she touched herself. Squeezing her nipples like he'd done.

"Good girl," he said in a harsh tone. He sounded like he was losing control, just as she was.

Her head fell back with a cry as his finger slid in and out, too big and insistent but filling that needy ache as his tongue went back to worshiping the slit between her legs.

"Mmm." He murmured his approval against her hot aching flesh as he watched her touching herself. "That's a good girl. That's my sweet angel."

"Oh," she moaned.

His tongue flicked that hard pearl, and she let out a short scream.

"That's right. I'm going to bring you close to heaven, Angel.

He sucked the hard nub between his teeth, and lights exploded behind her eyes. Her head thrashed from side to side as he burrowed between her thighs and kissed her, licked her, drove his finger harder and deeper inside her until—

"Oh God!" she shrieked as the world exploded around her, and she shattered into a million pieces.

His low chuckle brought her back to earth as he straightened her clothes and helped her sit upright.

"Not a god, love," he said, his voice smug even though his expression was tight. "Just a duke."

With a guilty glance, she spotted his hardness. "Are you in pain?"

"Yes," he said simply. "But tasting your sweet core was worth it."

Her cheeks were definitely on fire now, and his answering chuckle should have irked her. But before she could get angry, he pulled her into his arms and settled her cheek to his chest. "Don't worry, Angel. One day soon, you'll be begging me to claim you, so I won't be in pain for long."

She thought about telling him he was wrong. But as her eyes closed and her body reveled in the aftermath of whatever this was...

She wasn't quite sure that was true.

CHAPTER ELEVEN

RAFF'S BRIDE WOULD not so much as look at him.

Even now as they waited beside the carriage, her gaze slid away from his. Fetching, as always, in a soft green gown and bonnet, she looked just as innocent and sweet as she was.

And he, in his black jacket and scowl, felt like the very devil.

"Are you certain you wish to join me?" he asked. Again.

Truly, he hadn't expected her to wish to join him on his day-long excursion to see the new Earl of Foster. He'd offered for her to accompany him out of courtesy, but he'd been itching for some relief.

Besides, he couldn't let Benedict wallow alone in that miserable house for too long with only his grieving mother for company.

He offered Evangeline his hand to help her into the carriage, and she blushed prettily as she took it, stepping gracefully up into the vehicle.

His vow to keep from bedding her until she came to him had been a moment of sheer stupidity. This was clear to him now. It had been his pride talking, but after tasting her sweet sex the other night, after knowing full well how she sounded when she found release…

He looked away from her with a grunt of displeasure.

He might have been the devil, but he'd cast himself into hell.

Once the carriage was underway, his lovely bride seemed entranced by the view passing by. Nothing exciting to speak of—just trees and meadows, broken up occasionally by the odd winding creek. But Evangeline wore a soft smile as she took it all in.

And Raff, God help him, took her in.

He couldn't seem to look away, even though staring at her had become an act of torture.

His sweet bride was a stubborn little thing. Mysterious, too. In the days that had passed since their night in the kitchen, he'd grown more and more mystified by her.

One moment she'd be smiling and laughing, the next blushing and stammering. One moment he'd be convinced she was avoiding him, the next, she was seeking him out.

He could not understand her.

He hated how much he wanted to.

She chose that moment to glance over, and another pretty blush stole into her cheeks.

Was that because of what he'd done to her? Had he pushed her too far, too fast by tasting her like he had?

The thought made him scowl.

"Have you and Lord Foster been friends for long?" she asked suddenly.

He blinked in surprise and then stared some more when her blush deepened. How curious. What was going on in that mind of hers that asking such a mundane question made her blush?

"Since our school days," he said. A smile tugged at his lips as his mind wandered back to those early days when he and Benedict, along with Hayden and Malcolm, had first become friends. After so many years alone with only tutors and the occasional visit from his mother or father, it had felt like a new world opening when he'd discovered other children his age.

"That must be nice," she said. "To have such close friends."

He studied her anew, not missing the faraway look in her eyes. "Were there not many children your age around you?"

She shook her head. "I'm sure there were some in the nearest town, but out in the country, there were few neighbors, and until Baron Foley took over the neighboring estate, there were none near my age."

Her gaze dipped, and her cheeks reddened.

Something about this blush had his gut twisting ominously. Her expression wasn't one of shyness but guilt.

"It must have been nice to have school friends," she added quickly.

"Yes," he agreed. "It made it difficult to come back to the country estate during breaks."

She blinked up at him in surprise. "So, the county estate…that was where you were raised? That was your home?"

His smile felt cold. "I suppose you could say that."

Home to him conjured images of a life he'd never known. A family he'd never had. He glanced out the window to avoid her curious gaze.

"Were you lonely?" Her words were so soft, so full of sympathy.

A tight knot formed in his throat. His silence stretched too long, and so he forced himself to smile over at her. "I had friends."

His words only made that sympathy in her eyes deepen.

Bloody hell. He didn't need this girl's pity.

"I was lonely, too," she whispered.

His rising irritation died a sudden and swift death. His heart fell with a splat in his chest. The sincerity in her voice wasn't just laden with sympathy—it was understanding.

For one moment, their eyes connected, and he was sure he could feel it. A tie between them that had nothing to do with the physical pull he always experienced when she was near and everything to do with that look in her eyes.

"I'm sorry," he said.

She arched her brows. "That's the second time you've apologized to me, Your Grace. I'm not certain what to make of that."

His lips hitched up in a rueful grin. Her use of his title had been teasing. Almost like a friend poking fun. "I wouldn't get used to it," he muttered.

She laughed. The sound was lighter than wind chimes and more soothing than a lullaby. "You never did explain what you were apologizing for that last time."

He stilled. The gleam in her eyes held more than just curiosity. There was something close to hope there. Like his answer was important. He drew in a deep breath. He'd told her he didn't regret claiming her as his bride—and this was the truth.

Even knowing she wasn't the simple woman he'd thought she would be, he wasn't sorry he'd claimed her.

He leaned back. No, that wasn't right either. He was grateful for what he'd done precisely because she wasn't biddable and simple.

The thought left him temporarily speechless.

It wasn't until he saw her expectant smile falter that he realized he'd been silent too long.

"I told you I didn't regret marrying you, and that's the truth," he said, his voice firmer than intended. "And I don't regret keeping you from your would-be suitor either."

The last of her smile faded at the mention of her lover.

"If he hadn't the courage to claim you for himself, then he didn't deserve you," he said.

Her lips were pressed together in a thin line now, but she didn't look away. Did she agree?

That was likely too much to hope. But maybe one day, she'd see that any man who truly loved her would never have let her go.

He would certainly never let her go.

The mere thought had a roiling rage ripping through his insides, and his fists gripped the seat's edge beneath him until he came back to his senses. When he did, he found Evangeline blinking rapidly—whatever she'd seen in his expression shocking her thoroughly.

He cleared his throat as he tried to recall his point. *Ah, yes.* His apology. "I am sorry, however, if I caused a rift between you and your parents. You were close, I gather, and—"

"We weren't," she interrupted abruptly.

"Pardon?"

Her cheeks pinkened again, and she gave a helpless shrug. "Do not misunderstand me. I love my parents, but I would not say we were close."

He stared. He couldn't help it. The way she was speaking to him—he'd never heard this voice from her. It was raw and honest and—

Oh hell. He wanted to pull her into his arms when her eyes softened with emotion.

"I wish we were. I'd like to be. But I've always had this sense that I'm…" She paused to swallow. "A disappointment."

Rage unlike anything he'd ever known had him stiffening, his jaw clenching. "Surely not," he managed.

He wanted to kill her father. If that bloody viscount were here right now, Raff might. No one should ever make their daughter feel that way, especially not Evangeline.

Her smile was rueful. "I'm afraid so. The only way I did not fail them was…" She gestured to herself with a fluttering hand.

"Your beauty," he said for her.

She blushed anew.

Lord, but he could not get enough of her blushes. He itched to tug down the maddeningly demure neckline of her gown to see just how far that blush spread. Did it reach all the way to her perfect rosy buds?

He nearly groaned as his mind filled with the image of her bared breasts. What he wouldn't give to have her in his arms now, her perfect tits in his mouth as his hands stroked the soft flesh between her thighs.

"I'm afraid my demeanor has always been a disappointment, however," she was saying.

He came back to the moment with a start. "How could that

possibly be true?" he said. "You are honest and forthright. Shy, perhaps, but that only speaks to your modesty and your kind heart."

She stared at him like he was a ghost. "Do you...do you honestly think so?" Her hands fidgeted in her lap. "You don't think my lack of social decorum to be a hindrance as your...as your duchess?"

His heart melted right then and there. "Angel, you will make the perfect duchess. I told you already I don't care about social niceties. All I care about is—"

You. He stopped short before it could slip out. It wasn't true, obviously. He didn't care about this girl.

He stared at her, and she stared back.

Oh, bloody hell. When had he begun to care?

She arched her brows slightly as his silence grew too long.

"All I care about is siring an heir," he finished.

The words tasted like ash, and her sad smile made his chest ache.

"Of course," she murmured.

The moment he'd spoken, he wished he could call back the words.

But it was too late.

The rest of the journey passed in silence.

HOURS LATER, RAFF leaned back in his chair as he and Benedict watched the dowager countess lead Evangeline away for a tour of the newly rebuilt wing of the house.

Benedict wasted no time before turning to him to say, "You do know you're mad for the girl, don't you?"

Raff winced, but he couldn't bring himself to deny it.

He'd been coming to the same conclusion, and his friend had always been more attuned to such things. He supposed that was what came from growing up amidst a family.

He looked around the dark room with its shuttered windows and thick layer of dust.

Which was worse, to have a family and lose them or to never know that comfort in the first place?

A glance at Benedict's scarred face and dark eyes told Raff he was the lucky one here. His gaze drifted toward the door where his wife had just departed.

Perhaps he was the fortunate one, but right about now, he felt like a man condemned.

"She doesn't feel the same," he finally admitted.

"Are you certain about that?"

Raff nodded. "There's another."

"She's young," Benedict said. "She'll get over it. At some point, she'll likely thank you for saving her from a fate worse than death with that Foley fellow."

Raff froze. Foley. He'd heard the name before. With a jolt, he made the connection. That was the neighboring family Evangeline had mentioned. But how…

He glared at his friend. "How do you know about him?"

Benedict laughed, and the sound was harsh and grated due to his injured throat.

"You might not have cared to know anything about your fiancée in your mad dash to wed," Benedict said as he leaned back in his chair. "But Malcolm, Hayden, and I were not so lackadaisical about the matter. We weren't about to let you wed some callous harlot or some amoral chit who was bound to break your heart with her infidelities."

Raff scoffed on instinct. "Break my heart," he muttered under his breath. As if the thought was inconceivable.

As if it wasn't inevitable.

His chest tightened painfully as he avoided Benedict's all-seeing stare.

"You might be able to fool all of society, Raff, but we've known you too long," he said. "You want a family. You want a home."

Raff didn't deny it, but he didn't agree either. Was that what he wanted? Possibly. But only in the way that young girls like Evangeline wanted romance. It was a youthful ideal gone horribly awry. A childish notion that didn't exist in the real world.

He knew that.

Didn't he?

A silence fell as Raff went to war with himself over what he'd honestly expected from a marriage. Had he been hoping for family?

Bloody hell.

And Evangeline...

Why had he not gotten to know her? Why had he been so intent on keeping her pegged as some mindless, simple woman?

He'd wanted her to be simple. Had needed it to be so. Why was that?

He was glad she wasn't, it turned out. But her personality had come as a surprise—all of it.

He now knew that his wife was stubborn. She was timid, yes, but also brave in her own way—there were few men who'd dared to defy him the way she had. But most of all, she was kind.

He dropped his head into his hands. If his heart hadn't been melting with each new encounter with his wife, he would have lost the organ entirely after seeing her with Benedict today.

She'd been the very image of saintly kindness. A true angel. She hadn't so much as blinked in the face of his scars. She'd been nothing but gentle tenderness, even toward his unbearable mother, her sympathy in the face of the woman's grief a palpable thing.

Watching her today, he knew it. She was all that was good in the world.

And she was his.

But her heart...

Her heart belonged to some nitwit named Foley.

"Who is he? What sort of understanding did they share?" It

killed him to ask.

He wanted to believe his wife, but it was only now dawning on him how little he knew of her.

He was starting to know her—her person. Her heart. But her past? Her wishes? Her plans? A growl slipped out that made Benedict laugh.

Twice in one day, it seemed his bitter, angry friend just needed a fool to laugh at. Here they'd been trying to ply him with whores and liquor, but in the end, he'd just needed Raff to suffer to find amusement.

"You truly knew nothing of the man?" Benedict asked.

Raff sniffed. "Not until our wedding night."

Benedict tipped his head back with a loud laugh that startled a maid bustling about in the corner.

"What's he like?" Raff demanded. "What did he have to offer?"

"Nothing," Benedict said, sobering quickly. "Not a goddamn thing. I thought that was why you were so quick to steal her away. Hayden actually suggested you have some sort of chivalrous knight complex beneath that cold exterior."

Raff sneered. "Of course, I don't."

Benedict chuckled. "That's what I said."

Raff had more questions than he could manage, so he reached for his brandy. "So?" he demanded. "He's poor?"

"Not just that," Benedict said, his lips curving up in a sneer of disdain. "Poverty might be overlooked. But his family is…" Benedict shook his head. "There's nothing good there. The father is said to be cruel. The eldest brother married for money and by ungentlemanly means." He arched a brow meaningfully.

"He ruined a lady?"

Benedict grunted.

"The younger son, a Mr. Albert Foley…" Benedict's gaze followed in Evangeline's wake meaningfully. "He's said to be even more unscrupulous than his brother."

Raff stared into the fire as his heart thudded painfully in fury on his wife's behalf. What had been Foley's plan when it came to her?

Did he not know that her father was penniless? He couldn't have.

"Will you tell her?" Benedict said.

Raff gave a quick shake of his head. Poor thing had been through enough these past weeks thanks to him and his high-handed, selfish ways.

She'd been right that he hadn't given her wishes a single thought. Granted, he'd truly believed her father had been manipulating the situation, even lying to eke out more money from him. But all the same, he should have gone to her directly.

He should have courted her.

She deserved a man who tried, at the very least.

Self-disgust had him sinking into his seat as Benedict watched him closely. "What will you do?"

Raff shook his head. "No idea."

His challenge to her had been a stupid idea. He should have just taken her and then spent these past weeks wooing her in bed, showing her just how much he adored her by worshiping her body.

But no. He'd gone and thrown down a gauntlet, and now she had no reason to let him near.

And yet…

He shifted as a flicker of hope sparked in his chest.

And yet, she had let him close. Even today in the carriage, he suspected she was trying.

She was trying where he was not.

"See, Benedict?" he said when he realized he'd been too quiet. "This is why Hayden and I need you back in London. Malcolm might be fine and good with his betrothed, but Hayden and I need your help. You can't keep hiding away here."

Benedict's brows arched. "Haven't you heard?"

"Heard what?"

His friend's scarred features hardened. "Malcolm's betrothed ran away."

Raff straightened in his seat. "What?"

"Malcolm's beside himself, as you can imagine. Of course, this is just between us." He glanced pointedly toward the door where his mother and Evangeline had disappeared.

"Of course." Raff frowned. "But why? How?"

Benedict shrugged. "He's off trying to find her now, and when he finds her hopefully, he will get his answers." His brows drew down. "If it's not too late."

A somber silence fell. Raff had never met Malcolm's fiancée, but from what he'd heard, she was a quiet, obedient sort. The dutiful only daughter of a well-respected viscount. To think she might have run off with another or been ruined in some way…

This was disconcerting. There were few things in life that one could rely on, and Malcolm's marriage to Miss Lillian Grant was one of them.

"Did she run from him or—"

"He doesn't know," Benedict said.

"Is there anything I can do to help?"

Benedict shook his head. "For now, he's asked that we make his excuses. He does not wish for this to become common knowledge."

"Of course," he muttered.

"Besides," Benedict added with a knowing smirk. "It seems to me you have your own bride to worry about."

Raff gave a grunt of rueful amusement. "I do rather have my hands full at the moment."

"Do you want my advice?" Benedict said.

"Of course." He looked to his friend whose scars went so much deeper than those cuts that ran along his cheek and jaw.

"Tell her how you feel," Benedict said.

Raff scoffed. "I can't do that. She's already one foot out the door. I'd only scare her off."

"I think she's stronger than you know," his friend said, his low voice grave as sin. "But if you can't tell her, then show her."

Show her? Raff's mind went back to all the ways he would worship her body. If she let him. He scrubbed a hand over his eyes with a groan. If she begged him.

He could be waiting an eternity for that day to come.

"I don't know how to show her," he finally admitted.

"What does she like?" Benedict asked. "What does she want? Give her that."

He made it sound so simple. What did she want? Romance, he suspected. To be seen and valued and appreciated in the way her parents and society never had.

The fact that he knew that with such certainty was alarming.

The fact that he suspected she knew him just as well was even more terrifying.

"Figure that out and then give it to her," Benedict said.

Raff nodded slowly. "That…that I might be able to do."

He looked toward the door where she'd left with Benedict's mother. What was taking them so long? She'd been gone too long.

Funny, he'd been alone all his life, it seemed, but a few weeks with this woman, and he couldn't bear to have her out of his sight. "I'd best go find her. We ought to leave if we want to be back before sundown."

"One last thing," Benedict said when he went to leave.

Raff turned back expectantly.

Benedict smirked. "Don't mess this up."

CHAPTER TWELVE

E VANGELINE HAD NO patience left to spare. "That will be all, thank you."

She forced a smile as she sent the maids away, so she might find some reprieve with a bath.

Bathing had always calmed her in the past. Besides, it gave her something to do.

Not that she was bored, necessarily. How could she be when Raff had taken such measures to make sure she was occupied and entertained every minute of the day?

No, she was not bored. Just…restless.

Again.

She sank into the steaming water and let her head fall back against the tub's edge.

Restless again. Always.

She shivered despite the heat, her hands idly gliding over her too-sensitive skin.

What was the matter with her? She'd never been so unsettled before. And this unease had nothing to do with Raff. How could she complain about his actions when he'd been the perfect gentleman these past few days, since they'd visited his friend, the Earl of Foster.

Poor man.

She sank further into the water with a frown at the memory

of that tragic gentleman and his mother. So much sadness. So much grief.

And yet, she'd enjoyed her time there. Very much. It was her first time seeing Raff interact with anyone aside from her and a handful of servants who treated him like some god. But watching Lord Foster tease him and laugh with him as a friend—it had been eye-opening.

And watching Raff with Lord Foster—that had been enlightening as well.

She wasn't sure she could ever view Raff as the cold, unemotional duke any longer, not after seeing how much he cared. Oh, he covered it well as any gentleman would. He did not fawn or coo like a lady might have over an injured, grieving friend. But he'd been protective and thoughtful. Kind, in his own way.

She frowned now, splashing her fingers a bit as her mind tried to untangle the knot it had created this past fortnight.

They were set to leave on the morrow, back to London. She ought to be glad for the fact that she'd see her parents again. Perhaps even Albert, though she knew now, she would never take him up on his offer to save her. She supposed she'd always known it was not truly an option, but now it was not even a vague possibility to dream about.

Raff might have his faults. Indeed, he'd shown them all to great effect in the way he'd claimed her like he was some medieval ruler. She huffed, but even as she tried to summon up her initial self-righteous anger, she felt it. This new stirring that she couldn't seem to stop.

It happened whenever thoughts of Raff came to mind. Angry or affectionate, it didn't seem to matter. Her body reacted the same way.

Even now, she looked down at her naked body to see her nipples hardening, and lower, there was a deep, insistent ache forming between her thighs.

An ache that hadn't been relieved since that night in the kitchen when he'd pressed his mouth to her entrance. When he'd made love to her so skillfully with his tongue and hands.

Her head dropped back with a gasp at the memory.

But it was another memory that had her hand skimming down her body, over her breasts, and sliding slowly toward the curls that covered her *mons*.

He'd shown her how to find relief.

She could do it now. She bit her lip. Couldn't she?

"Evangeline?" The duke's voice calling her name made her start, and water sloshed over the sides.

His voice was close, right next to the adjoining door that led to his bedroom.

She ought to tell him she was bathing. She should say "stay out." But instead, she heard herself say, "Come in."

He opened the door and stopped short. The change in him was instant, and it put that earlier ache to shame.

Need was a desperate, clawing monster in her lower belly, begging to be touched and adored. Her skin tingled and burned everywhere his gaze fell.

And it fell everywhere.

In a heartbeat, he took her in, from head to toe. The darkness in his eyes when they met hers should have been frightening. It wasn't just desire; it was lust. It was possessive, and it was brutal. It was merciless.

If she had any sense of self-preservation, she would send him away. But she couldn't. She didn't want to.

A wolf peered at her with hungry eyes, but in that moment, she knew.

She understood.

Her heart was hammering in her chest, and her hands trembled. But there was no fear there. Not even a flicker of terror.

He would not hurt her.

The knowledge flooded her with courage. More than that, she felt dangerous. She wanted to push. She wanted to tease.

She felt...

She felt...

What was this feeling?

Slowly. Ever so slowly, she stood. Water sloshed, and her breathing was too loud, too shaky.

But as his gaze raked over her and she jutted her breasts out for his perusal, her hands sliding over herself in a way that made him groan…

This was power.

She'd had a taste of it once before, but that was nothing compared to this. Because now she knew what she did to him. What was more, she knew with certainty that she was safe with this man. He might push, and he might taunt, but he would never take what she was unwilling to give.

He would never hurt her.

His lust made her ache, yes, but it also made her chest swell and her spine straighten.

His desire for her was heady. She'd missed it these past few days when he'd been such a gentleman. Kind, polite…but distant.

He hadn't let her see any of this animalistic desire. And oh, Lord, how she'd missed it.

"You're playing with fire, Angel," he growled.

She smiled. She couldn't help it. She knew precisely what she was doing.

"I trust you," she whispered.

He looked nearly as shocked by that admission as she felt.

And what it did to his gaze… His eyes grew darker still. But softer somehow, that lust tempered with affection.

It made her heart ache just as much as that place between her thighs.

She meant it. She trusted him not to touch her no matter how tempted he might be. He'd made a vow, and he wouldn't break it.

His gaze followed a drop of water that was traveling down her neck. She looked down, too, and they both watched as it hovered on the tip of her nipple.

She peeked up at him, and the air rushed out of his lungs.

He was a man transfixed, his gaze so intense it was as though the fate of the world rested on that little droplet of water.

Meanwhile, she had this weighted feeling. A knowledge, really—that the fate of their marriage rested on this moment.

On her. And what she did next.

Would she continue to hold him at bay? Would she fight the inevitability of what was to come?

Or would she embrace her future?

Would she embrace *him*?

A flicker of fear rose up, but she squelched it with a deep breath, her hands fisting at her sides.

He noticed the change in her and finally tore his gaze from her tight, needy nipples to meet her gaze.

"Raff," she whispered. "This is me…begging."

She held her breath as he stilled. The hunger in his eyes was like nothing she'd ever seen. For a moment, she doubted herself.

For a second, she was scared.

But then he strode toward her and scooped her into his arms, lifting her easily and holding her wet body tightly to his chest. The fear was replaced with a desire so sudden and so hot, she forgot how to breathe.

His voice was gruff, but his hold was gentle as he held her to him. "There's no turning back now, love."

Love. The word lingered in the air between them. Just a term of endearment, and one he'd used before, but it still wrapped around her now and gave her strength.

She lifted a hand and cupped his cheek with her palm.

He growled soft and low, but he pressed into her trembling touch.

"You're my husband," she said simply. "And I am ready to make this a *real* marriage."

CHAPTER THIRTEEN

RAFF WASTED NO more time.

Weeks' worth of pent-up desire had his mouth claiming hers in a hot, open, hungry kiss before he'd reached the bed.

Even when his knees bumped against the edge, he found himself reluctant to let go of the wet, wanton creature in his arms.

She wrapped her arms around his neck and pressed those perfect tits against him. Wet as she was, she soaked the fabric of his shirt, and through it, he could feel all of her. Her hot skin, her hard nipples, the softness of her thighs.

He groaned as his fingers dug into her flesh, holding her tighter before finally setting her down gently atop the bed.

For a long moment, he ignored the primal need that had his manhood standing at attention and forced himself to wait. To devour her with his eyes before climbing atop her.

Because once he had her in his arms, he'd be lost to desire, and right now, for one heartbeat, he wanted to see her. All of her.

"Beautiful." It came out choked and gruff. His lungs were too tight with reverence. With awe. His gaze roved over her bare belly that glistened with bath water, down to the swell of her hips, lingering at that dark tuft of curls—the only shield between her tight cunny and his hard shaft.

Her back arched slightly as if her tits were begging for attention.

A smile tugged at his lips at the thought. Those rosy nipples were hard, and the soft swell of her breasts were rising and falling quickly.

His gaze darted up to her face. Was she afraid?

His tension eased the moment he caught her dazed gaze locked on his groin. She bit her lip, but it wasn't fear he saw there. It was curiosity.

Maybe a little trepidation, too.

He stepped closer and reached for her hand, bringing it down to cover his hard length. With his hand over hers, he cupped her fingers around his shaft, groaning when she gasped.

With wide eyes, she glanced up at him.

"It's all right, Angel," he said. "I don't want you to be frightened, and you can't hurt me."

She wet her lips, and he bit back another groan. This was temptation like he'd never known. The most beautiful woman in the world spread out for him like a buffet, willing and eager and his.

His for the taking.

Once again, he had to inhale deeply against the tightening in his chest.

He was humbled by the moment. Him. A duke who'd never been humble about anything in his life. But eyeing this woman who was his to bed. His to worship. His to…

He shook off the thought before it could finish.

No.

He would not love her.

She shifted onto her side, adjusting her grip on his cock. The innocence in her gaze when she peeked up at him through her lashes was nearly his undoing. "Are you certain I cannot hurt you?"

Her grip was so light, and yet he throbbed in her hand at the sound of her voice.

"I'll show you how to touch me, shall I?"

Hell. He felt like this was his first time. He'd never been with a virgin before. The enormity of what he was about to do—of what *they* were about to do—struck him anew.

She was his wife. She was his to take care of. Her happiness, her pleasure…it rested in his hands.

She nodded. "Yes, please."

He shucked off his shirt, followed by his breeches, his gaze never wavering from hers. He gave her a moment to stare at his member, despite the fact that her wide-eyed gaze and those sweetly parted lips had his heart pounding with the exertion of holding back.

She gave him her hand, the gesture so trusting he swore right then and there to never take her trust for granted. To never give her reason to look at him the way she had their first night together.

He settled her hand over his length and let go.

She gasped, biting her lip as a blush stole over her cheeks. With tentative fingers, she explored the ridge at the head, then traced her fingers up and down the rigid length.

This was hell.

It was torture.

And yet…he couldn't look away.

"Angel," he said, his voice thick with unbridled lust. "You won't hurt me, but I…" He let out a sharp exhale. "I'm afraid there's no way around me causing you some pain. I'll do my best to be gentle, but—"

"I know," she said softly.

"You do?"

With a soft smile, she said, "My mother told me that part."

"Ah. Er… What else did she tell you?"

Her eyes glittered with laughter as she blushed bright red. "Well, she did not tell me about any of the things you've already done to me. And she never mentioned how good it felt when I…that is, when you…"

He leaned down, cupping her cheeks in his hands to kiss her.

She kissed him back so sweetly, it brought another tightening in his chest. A warmth spreading through him that had nothing to do with the heat of passion which had his loins throbbing, begging for release.

Her mouth opened for him readily, her tongue sliding to meet his, tangling and tasting with an eagerness that made his heart soar.

This was night and day compared to the way their wedding night had gone. Everything about it was different. Better. Not just her physical response, but the way she looked at him with trust, the way she lay back and reached her arms out to him.

Almost as if she really were begging.

As if she were just as eager to satisfy this aching need as he was.

He settled himself over her and tried to show her instead, his lips covering her cheeks and jaw in gentle kisses as he trailed a light caress over her arms, her waist.

He gave her time to adapt to the newness of it all.

Yes, they'd been intimate in the past, but never like this. She'd never been naked beneath him, at his mercy. Her stomach muscles tightened as his fingers made lazy circles over her ribs and lower belly.

"You're teasing me," she said in a breathless whisper.

He chuckled before claiming her lips in another deep, languid kiss. "You've been teasing me for weeks, Angel. I'd say it's only fair."

She opened her mouth to retort but gasped instead as her hips arched off the bed to meet his fingers as he slid them down between her thighs. "You like it when I touch you there, love?"

"Yes." Her whisper was harsh, and he grinned down at her in response.

He ground his hardness into her hip with a quick thrust. "Do you feel what you do to me? Do you have any idea how long I've lain awake at night imagining this very moment?"

She batted her lashes, her lips parting. "What did you do

about it?"

Her eyelids were growing heavy, and there was no mistaking the dark glimmer that filled her gaze.

"Naughty, naughty girl," he whispered against her ear. "Do you want to see how I took myself in hand, pretending it was your tight little cunny?"

She gasped at his vulgarity, but with a quick flick of her tongue to wet her lips, she turned her head to meet his gaze. "Yes."

He reached for her hand again. "How about I show you?"

Her breathing quickened as he once more brought her hand to his shaft and used her grip to stroke himself until they were both breathing heavily.

After a bit, he released his hold, and she kept going. Soon, she even grew brave enough to broaden her exploration, her fingers gently touching his thighs and ballocks as he teased her folds with strokes of his own.

"Lord, but you are wet," he growled as his fingers parted her lips and found the liquid heat at her core. He dipped a finger inside her, making her whimper before drawing it back out, spreading her wetness as he slid his fingers through her folds.

He dipped his head, nibbling at the sensitive skin of her neck and then lower. Lower still.

She cried out, her head arching back as his lips covered her nipple and sucked it.

He sucked hard, his tongue teasing one tip and then the other. She forgot her own exploration as she brought her hands up to hold his head to her breasts, her hips wriggling beneath him. "Please," she whimpered when he teased her entrance but pulled away when she arched up to meet him. "Please, please."

His lips curled up in a smile as he let his teeth graze over her hard nipple.

She moaned his name.

Triumph had his hands growing more confident. More urgent. She might have said she was begging before, but this…

"Raff, please," she moaned.

His name was a plea on her lips, and he could hold back no longer.

Positioning himself between her thighs, he nudged her entrance. The temptation to slam into her tight heat was almost more than he could bear. But stronger than that was an urge to protect her, even from himself.

He hesitated, sweat breaking out on his brow as he hovered over her, his weight resting on his forearms, so he didn't crush her.

"I don't want to hurt you," he said.

She lifted her head to kiss him. "I know." She rocked her hips, bringing her hot entrance in contact with his rock-hard member. "But I want this." She rested her head back down, and her big blue eyes met his with sweet, open honesty. "I want to be your wife."

He groaned as he kissed her, her words wrapping around him and making his slow thrust into her entrance feel like a momentous occasion.

Her hot breath against his lips was a pant, a whimper.

I want to be your wife.

You are my husband.

He was just as bowled over by this woman's words as he was by the perfection of her body.

And she was perfect.

She was tight, and he eased into her slowly, pausing to let her adjust to him. Each time he paused, he worshiped her with kisses. He used his tongue to tease her ear, her neck. He dipped his head to suck on those perfect tits until she wiggled restlessly beneath him. A silent plea for more.

She cried out and stilled beneath him when he broke through her virgin barrier, but after another long moment of kisses and whispered words of praise and encouragement, she tilted her hips, and he was fully sheathed.

He was home.

Not thrusting, not taking, not claiming her with rough hard movements strained his every muscle. Every instinct begged him to bed her hard. To bring her to climax so fast, he drove out any memory of any other man. To claim her and fill her with his seed. To make her his so no one else could ever have her.

This wave of possessiveness rocked him to his core. But through it all, he held still. He kissed her and stroked her as she slowly softened beneath him, her breathing evening as her impossibly tight channel made room for him.

"Angel," he groaned against her neck as he slowly shifted inside her, letting her get used to the friction. "You feel so good."

"You feel…odd," she said. She gave a breathless laugh, and he chuckled, too.

Never in his life had he thought he might laugh during sex— and certainly not with his wife.

But that soft laughter made the moment even more significant.

He pulled his head back to meet her soft, languid gaze. "You are my wife," he said. "And I am so grateful to be your husband."

Her eyes welled with unshed tears before she blinked them away. Then she reached up and buried her fingers in his hair to drag his mouth down to hers for a long, deep kiss. When she released him, they were both breathless, and he thought he might explode with the effort it took to be so still inside her.

"I'm ready," she whispered against his lips, her hips moving restlessly.

He chuckled. "Mmm, *now* you're ready, are you?" He nipped at her neck. "After teasing me for so long? Tell me what you want, Angel. Tell me what you need."

With a gasp, she arched her hips upward as she sought friction and relief. "I want…I need…" Her breaths were short and choppy as she wriggled beneath him. "Take me," she said the words a whimper. A plea.

He growled against her soft skin. "You want more, is that it?" He rocked against her, and she moaned with pleasure.

"Yes. More," she gasped.

A smile tugged at his lips as he kissed her. "Greedy girl."

She giggled, the sound so sweet it tore his heart out. "You're the one who called me Angel. I never made any such claim."

"Mmm," he agreed with a grin as he pulled out slightly and then drove back in. She gasped again, but this was one of pleasure, and her muscles clenched around him tight.

"It seems I was mistaken. You're no angel at all, are you?" he teased as she rocked her hips again, trying to claim more of him.

"Not an angel," she agreed with a pant as he drove into her harder than before. Her grin was outright wicked as she dug her fingers into his back. "Not an angel," she panted again. "Just your wife."

CHAPTER FOURTEEN

I T WAS SO silly to be nervous.

Evangeline was well aware that she was being utterly ridiculous, and yet she could not make her belly stop quivering with nerves as she toyed with the food on her plate.

"We don't have to go, of course," Raff said from the far end of the table.

She blinked. What was he on about? It was hard to say what with their sitting so far apart and all. Unlike at the country estate, the townhouse had one long dining room table, and his servants had set them so far apart it would have been comical if she were in the mood to laugh.

She was not, however, in a highly laughable mood.

"To the Bermans' ball tomorrow night?" he said, arching a brow and holding up an invite in such a way that she felt certain he'd said as much at least twice before.

"Oh, yes," she said, forcing a smile. "I have no preference."

This was a lie. What was more, it was a lie, and they both knew it.

She wasn't sure why she'd said it, to be honest, but it had Raff's gaze growing even more distant than before.

Or maybe that was just the physical distance between them, and she was overreacting.

She set her knife down and gulped. This would not do. Only

last night she'd felt closer than ever with her husband. Indeed, he'd held her in his arms, and he'd murmured soft words, meaningless but sweet, until she'd fallen asleep.

But that was last night.

And today, everything was different.

It had been different since the moment she'd woken up in her bedroom of the country estate—alone. She'd then been hurried along by her lady's maid to ready herself for the morning's journey back to London.

She'd known they were returning, of course, but she hadn't expected everything to feel so very different upon her return.

She glanced over at an unfamiliar footman who stood guard by the doorway.

Perhaps it was the fact that this was a new home, with all new people. Her gaze returned to her husband, who was still sorting through all the correspondence that had been waiting for them—for him, rather—upon their return.

All invitations. All for society events that she typically avoided. Which he knew.

And yet, she'd felt compelled to lie and say she had no opinion. Why?

But she knew why. His words and hers from the night before had not ceased haunting her all day. Their vows in front of God felt like nothing compared to last night's act.

She squeezed her thighs together as an ache filled her anew at the memory. An ache...and soreness. All day she'd been uncomfortable between her legs, and even now, she kept shifting in her seat to find relief.

But last night... Well, last night, there had been pain, yes, but it had been so far overshadowed by pleasure that pain had been an afterthought. A slight nagging twinge after the initial jolt of pain. And then he'd brought her to heights she hadn't even dreamed of. He'd petted her and stroked her and teased her with delicious kisses until she'd exploded with release.

Twice, in fact.

And now, today, they were here in London. Her parents were here as well, as was Albert. All people she should want to see, but she didn't, and she couldn't say why.

It was as if she'd been starting to come to some realization in the country. She'd been starting to feel like herself for the first time in a long time. She and Raff had even been finding common ground, getting to know each other the way a married couple ought.

And that was still the case.

Wasn't it?

Except, it didn't feel that way right now. A nagging sensation kept tugging at her belly, and no matter how she tried, she couldn't bring herself to eat.

She'd felt as though everything had changed the night before.

But now…

Had it?

Or was that her romantic nature painting a rosy glow over a practical event. He needed a sire, that was all. Nothing had changed. Not really.

Mercifully, he let the topic of the ball and all the other events that awaited fall by the wayside and instead filled her in on how this London home was run and who was in charge of what.

It felt every bit like the impersonal business arrangement this marriage had been in the first place. And perhaps still was?

After dinner, she wasn't certain what to do with herself, and so she retired to a foreign room in a house that felt like it was haunted.

Not with ghosts, though. Oh no, ghosts she could laugh off. It was more like the specters of lovers past that haunted the halls and seemed to live amongst the thick brocade curtains and the canopy over her bed.

How many women had her husband brought to this house? How many women had he pleasured the way he'd done to her?

"Stuff and nonsense," she muttered to herself as she brushed out her hair in front of the vanity. It wasn't as though he'd kept mistresses in the duchess's chambers.

She dropped the brush as she met her reflection with a furrowed brow.

He didn't, did he? And even if he had, she didn't care.

But would he again?

Of course he would. He'd told her as much, hadn't he? He'd said he'd take other lovers after she was with child.

Unless she claimed her spot in his bed, he'd said. Unless she decided she wanted to be the only one to satisfy his needs. That was what he'd said.

And she hadn't cared. She still didn't care if he had his needs satisfied elsewhere.

She sat and stared at her reflection as if her image might explain to her why she was lying to herself and what exactly it meant that the thought of Raff with other women felt like glass in her veins.

A knock on her door was a welcome interruption from her thoughts. And when Raff smiled at her in the doorway when she answered, some of that anxiety and fear faded.

"I hate to leave you alone on your first night here," he said by way of explanation for his presence.

She drew in a quick breath, her heart fluttering in her chest and her belly already heavy with eager anticipation. Mercy, but he'd made a hoyden of her. She was far too eager to feel his hands on her again, to try kissing him the way he'd done to her, to—

"But I really ought to leave you be," he finished with a sigh.

She frowned. "Why?"

His lips twitched. "Aren't you sore, Angel?"

Angel. The word twisted around her and made her warmer than she'd been all day. She was still his angel.

And his wife.

The thought helped to ease her earlier jealousy. And it was jealousy, she could admit that much. But he was her husband. It was only right she be protective of what was hers. "I am a little sore," she admitted.

His smile was knowing and tender, and it made her heart thud painfully. He leaned in, cupping the back of her head as he kissed her forehead. "Then I shall let you rest. For now." He wore a wicked grin when he pulled back.

"Raff," she said, stopping him when he went to walk away.

"Yes?"

"About tomorrow…" She swallowed, not even certain what she wished to say. She felt inexplicably needy. Like a child, she wished for reassurances of some sort. She swallowed back a sigh of irritation with herself. "Never mind."

"Do you not wish to go to the ball, love?" His voice was so gentle. So understanding.

Had she ever thought him a cold, unfeeling cad? It was almost hard to reconcile her initial impressions with the man she'd come to know these past weeks.

She felt torn down the middle by such a simple question.

Did she wish to go and be seen by everyone? Be gawked at and whispered about? No. But when she imagined staying home alone. Of Raff attending without her. Of every female in attendance watching him with admiration.

Her gut twisted violently.

His brows drew together in concern. "What is it? You seem troubled. You have all day, in fact."

Her heart flipped in her chest at the questions in his eyes.

Did he think she regretted their time together last night?

Did he regret the things he'd said? The kindness and affection he'd shown her? Was he worried she would form an attachment that he did not want?

She let out a long, weary sigh. Her thoughts were running away from her, and she needed to get her head on straight. "It's disconcerting being here in a new environment…again."

His gaze softened with tenderness as he reached out and brushed her long hair back over her shoulder. "My apologies, Angel. I was not thinking about how difficult all this change must be for you."

Before she could agree or protest, he continued, taking a step back which left her feeling cold all over.

"I'm pushing you, aren't I?" He shook his head. "I know you are not fond of society outings, and I'd promised you that you would not be required to perform such duties as my duchess."

"Oh, that's not—"

"You should stay home," he said.

Like a child.

He hadn't said it. He hadn't even insinuated such a thing, but an inner voice chided her all the same.

"No," she said, perhaps too abruptly judging by his arched brows. "I want to go."

He stared at her for a long moment but finally tipped his chin in acknowledgment. "When the Season is over, you can return to the country if you wish."

Will you join me? The words hovered on her tongue, but she couldn't bring herself to ask.

She felt needy, and that neediness rankled. She didn't want to need his company. She didn't want to *want* it. And she certainly didn't want to see pity in his gaze when he told her once again that this marriage existed for one reason only—an heir.

He'd never pretended he wanted a real marriage or a family. She'd always dreamt of such a life, but not with him.

When had she started to dream of such a life with Raff?

He was watching her expectantly. She could leave for the country at the end of the Season. Most likely without him.

She nodded. "Very well."

He left her with a murmured goodnight. But no kiss. No passionate embrace.

She closed the door behind him with a sigh and climbed into her large, empty bed.

She'd see her parents at the ball, most likely. And Albert.

She waited to feel something. Anything. A pang of regret, a pang of remorse.

She felt…nothing.

With a frown, she stared up at the canopy that seemed to weigh down on her like a wet blanket. Why didn't she feel anything?

What did that say about her? About her feelings?

But the more she tried to call up her love for Albert, the more it felt like she was trying to catch hold of the fog. It slipped through her fingers, growing more and more hazy with each attempt.

The dreams she'd clung to for the past year, before her marriage, now felt like a childish dream.

Two weeks had passed, but it felt like a lifetime.

A future with Albert had never felt...real. It had been based on poetry and stolen touches. No real conversation. They'd never even shared a kiss.

Would Albert have taught her how to touch herself? Would he have been so very gentle when he claimed her as his wife?

She shook her head with an exasperated sigh. She couldn't imagine lying with Albert, and it felt wrong to even try.

It was disloyal to Raff. But it was more than that. She frowned up at the canopy as she sorted through her muddled emotions. And her *lack* of emotions.

Whatever it was she'd had with Albert felt completely inconsequential compared to the living, breathing, harsh, brutal, beautiful, passionate reality of living with Raff.

By the time sleep claimed her, Evangeline was only truly certain of one thing.

She'd never loved Albert. She'd merely wanted to be loved. She'd been desperate for it.

But what haunted her dreams and made her toss and turn was the question left in that realization's wake.

Was it the same with Raff?

Was she so desperate for love that she'd imagined his tenderness? Was he truly the man she wanted?

Or did she just long to be wanted?

CHAPTER FIFTEEN

HE SHOULD NEVER have brought her here.

Raff tried to keep his delectable bride in his sights, but the crush was unmanageable. It seemed everyone wanted a word with the new duchess.

"Married life suits you," Hayden said beside him. "Although, I'll admit I hadn't expected you to still be this smitten with the chit." He snapped his fingers in front of Raff's face. "Stop gawking at your own wife, man. It's embarrassing."

He turned his glare to his friend. "She's not some chit. She's my wife. My duchess. And she's currently being hounded by half of the guests at this party."

"She'll have to learn how to manage that," Hayden said with a shrug. "Might as well start tonight."

Hayden had a point, and Raff knew it. He couldn't fret over his wife like some nursemaid. She was a grown woman, as she was so quick to point out. She didn't need him fussing over her.

And yet...

"Hold my drink," he said, thrusting his glass in Hayden's direction.

"Wonderful," his friend intoned. "I finally have a friend to keep me company at one of these dreadful society events, and I'm left to hold his brandy."

Evangeline's mother reached her side, and he could practically see his angel's relief. He took his drink back, his attention returning to Hayden.

Wariness stole over him. Guilt, too. He'd been so lost in his own concerns, he'd nearly forgotten that Malcolm was contending with a runaway fiancée.

Hayden cut him a curious look.

"Has he found her yet?" Raff asked.

Hayden shook his head. "Haven't you heard?" Hayden wasn't drunk tonight—at least not visibly. Not yet. But his devil-may-care grin had been firmly in place until now.

Now his expression was alarmingly grim.

"Heard what?"

"Malcolm's father died."

"What?" Raff turned to his friend in shock. Not horror by any means. The old earl was as cruel as they came. His death would likely be welcome news.

But then again, the death of a parent, cruel or otherwise, must still be a blow.

"What happened?" he asked.

Hayden looked around to ensure they weren't being overheard. "I don't know the details. I imagine his death will be announced in all the papers tomorrow, but Malcolm didn't share many details in his missive. All I know is that there was an accident, and it somehow involved his bride-to-be. Malcolm said he'll be back once he'd dealt with the estate and legalities."

Raff exhaled loudly. "So Malcolm is the new Earl of Fallenmore."

"It would seem so."

Raff turned to him. "And his fiancée? Did he find her?"

Hayden arched a brow. "She'd left him for another, it would seem. I suspect there's a story there, but we'll have to wait until he's back to learn more."

Raff shook his head. "Lost his father and his bride-to-be. Poor Malcolm."

"Indeed."

To see Hayden so grim left Raff ill at ease. "What can we do?"

Hayden blew out a long sigh. "Not much until he returns. I imagine the scandal sheets and the newspapers will be all over this story."

Raff grunted. "Whatever he needs," he promised.

Hayden nodded. It had always been this way between the four of them. Little family to rely on, they could rely on each other.

They'd been Raff's only family until Evangeline. He turned to seek her out. His Evangeline, who was—

He frowned. Where was she?

He spotted her with her mother, still, but a gentleman was speaking to her. He was too close by far, and his smile far too ingratiating.

Instant dislike had Raff growling. His spine stiffened, and his muscles tightened as he spoke to Hayden without removing his gaze from his wife. "Who's that talking to Evangeline?"

Hayden craned his neck for a better look. "Oh him? He's that baron's second son. A fortune hunter, from the sounds of it. What's his name again..." He snapped. "Foley, that's it. Albert Foley."

Fire swept through Raff's blood and singed his lungs.

"Don't tell me you're jealous, old man," Hayden said with a laugh. But his laugh faded fast at whatever he saw on Raff's face. "She's your wife, Raff. And she's in good company." He leaned in closer and lowered his voice. "Don't go making a scene. She won't thank you for it."

"What do I care what she wishes?" he snapped, already moving away from his friend.

Hayden was right. He knew that. Some logical part of his brain was still functioning, but it was drowned out by a sickening roar of blood in his ears.

Jealousy.

Bloody hell, so this was what jealousy felt like.

He wasn't proud of himself as he reached her side and

claimed her arm, but he couldn't stop himself from glaring at the other man either. "If you'll excuse us," he said to no one in particular.

Evangeline gave a little squeak of surprise before falling into step beside him as he led her through the crowd.

"Where are we going?" she asked.

The alarm in her voice had him softening slightly. "We need to speak," he said. "In private."

She asked no more questions, and if she were frightened by the fact that he was dragging her into a darkened hall leading to the Bermans' private quarters, she kept silent.

It wasn't until he opened a door leading to a pitch-black room that she finally spoke.

"Raff, is…is something the matter?" Her voice was breathless.

Was that fear or guilt?

He rounded on her, clapping his hands against the door on either side of her head.

His sweet angel gazed up at him, blinking as her eyes adjusted to the darkness, moonlight spilling in behind him the only light by which to see.

"Was that your lover?" he demanded.

She gasped, her eyes widening…but she didn't deny it.

"He dared to speak to you when you are my wife?" He barely recognized his voice, it was laced with such rage.

He did not do anger. He'd never been given to fits of temper. Why would he be when he'd always had his way?

Anything he'd wanted, he'd gotten. Even her. His angel.

He'd snared her all right. He'd made her his duchess as he'd planned.

But was she his?

His heart slammed against his chest. Would she ever truly be his if she still loved another?

In an effort to calm himself, his gaze dipped down. She glowed in the moonlight. The bare skin of her decolletage a teasing glimmer of what he'd find if he tugged down her bodice.

His hand cupped her breast, making her gasp anew.

"Mine," he muttered through clenched teeth.

She nodded quickly. "Yours," she whispered. A trembling hand came up to touch his cheek, and for a moment, that overwhelming anger and jealousy was replaced by sanity.

She was his. He turned his face to kiss her palm, guilt warring with anger at having frightened her. He shut his eyes against a torrent of emotions he could not name.

Anger, yes. Jealousy, definitely. A possessive surge he'd never felt before. But something deeper. Stronger.

Something that had him tugging her into his arms, kissing her fiercely as if he might mark his claim with the force of his kiss.

His insides clenched as she opened for him willingly, her tongue meeting his with the same ferocity as a moan sounded from deep in her throat.

He had her pressed against the door now, her chest arching as she pressed her soft, warm breast into his grasping palm.

He ground his hardness into her soft belly, relishing in the sound of her whimper in his ear.

This was wrong, and he knew it. She was his wife. A lady. A duchess. He wasn't supposed to tup her hard in some back room of a ball like some tawdry whore.

"I want you, Angel," he rasped, his teeth bare against her neck as they ground together, trying to get closer.

"Then take me," she whispered.

He stilled, certain he'd heard wrong. When he pulled back, all he could see were her wet, swollen lips and her eyes, dark in the moonlight and lit with an emotion he couldn't name.

He didn't want to name it.

"He can never have you," he said, his voice harsher than intended.

She flinched, but her chin came up as she nodded. "I am yours, Raff. I know that. And I would never break my vows."

That weight of anger eased, but it wasn't enough. He gripped her chin, tilting her head back for another deep, searing kiss.

His other hand gripped her waist, and he pressed the full length of his body against hers.

He believed her. She was a good girl, a sweet young lady who didn't break her vows. Not even when he'd told her he had every intention of doing so once she was with child.

He pressed his forehead to hers, their labored breaths mingling as his hands gripped her skirts. "Are you wet for me, Angel?"

Her gasp thrust her tits upward, and he kissed the top of those luscious mounds as he made short work of hitching her skirts up to her waist. Her undergarments he ripped, eliciting another moan from his wife.

"Do you like it like that?" he asked. Disbelief filled his voice, but the moment his fingers slid between her folds, he had his answer.

"Yes," she hissed, her hips jerking as he thrust two fingers inside her dripping wet heat.

He nearly came right then and there in his breeches, like a youth at the feel of her excitement. "You like that you're mine, love?" he taunted.

"Y-yes," she breathed, her hips rolling as he slid his fingers in and out. With his free hand, he tugged down her bodice until her breasts spilled over, and he wasted no time taking a sweet nipple in his mouth to suckle.

She cried out, her hands in his hair, holding him close.

He suckled and fondled those lush, soft tits until she was moaning too loudly—so loudly they might be caught.

He didn't care. Not so long as she rode his fingers like a wanton mistress eager to ride his shaft.

"I'm going to take you right here and now," he promised, his lips close to her ear.

"Yes," she hissed again.

"I'm going to take what's mine," he added through gritted teeth.

She tugged on his hair to pull his head back, meeting his gaze.

"Yours."

It was a promise. Another vow. But as he released his cock from his breeches, as he drove it into her entrance ruthlessly, slamming her up against the wall and making her cry out with pleasure, he finally understood.

She'd given him her body, and she was too good to break that vow.

He wanted her body, yes, but he also wanted her heart and her soul.

He wanted all of her.

As she met his thrusts with frantic hip movements of her own, this reality slammed into him with a heartbreaking jolt.

He wanted all of her. Because she already owned all of him.

His body. His soul.

His bloody heart.

CHAPTER SIXTEEN

EVANGELINE HAD NEVER felt so wild. So wanton. She didn't even recognize herself as she grasped at Raff's neck, his shoulders, his hair.

Her legs were wrapped around his body, her body pinned against the door with each hard, merciless thrust of Raff's hips.

And it wasn't enough. She couldn't seem to get enough, even as he filled her so thoroughly, she felt like she might never walk again. He was hard and thick inside her, and with each new thrust, he seemed to bury himself deeper.

She welcomed it, but it wasn't enough. Physically, he owned her. Her inner muscles squeezed around him as she pressed her breasts closer, loving the friction as her nipples slid up and down against his shirt with each movement.

But it still wasn't enough. There was an ache in her chest. An emptiness that wasn't touched by the ruthless hammering as he had his way with her.

Why? What more did she want from him?

Her thoughts scattered like leaves on the wind when he reached between them and touched the hard nub at the top of her slit. She cried out, her hips bucking as she rode him hard and fast, her movements unskilled, no doubt, but pure instinct taking over.

His fingers ground into her bottom as he helped her, his other hand working her over furiously as he rammed into her over and over and—

"Raff!" She called his name as he drove into her one last time, her chest cracking open and her mind reeling as bliss washed through and left her limp.

She heard his groan and felt him pulse inside her as he found his release as well, and for a long moment, they collapsed there together, her arms wound tight around him as he rested his weight against her, holding her up against the door.

The door.

She stiffened as reality returned.

"Do you think anyone heard?" she asked.

She felt his grin against his neck. "Does it matter?"

When she didn't answer, he straightened with a sigh. "Likely not," he said. "There was music playing in the ballroom, and few would dare venture into private quarters."

"Only a duke," she teased.

His lips twitched slightly. "Or a mad man."

A silence fell, and more questions than she could handle rushed to her lips. Had he been jealous? Her heart started to race in her chest, a new sort of pleasure forming. Something light and sweet and…hopeful.

He pulled out of her and set her on her feet. Then he found a handkerchief and went to wipe her thighs, but she stopped him, taking it from him instead. "I'll take care of it."

He was silent as he watched her.

When she straightened her gown and reached up to try and tidy her hair, he put a hand on hers to stop her. "Leave it."

"But…" She swallowed hard. Without a mirror, she couldn't say for certain, but she suspected she looked as though she'd just been taken hard and rough. "Everyone will know."

His smirk was just barely visible in the moonlight. "That your new husband can't keep his hands off of you? I should think so. Now they'll know that you are mine."

"Was that what this was?" she asked, her voice so soft she was surprised he could hear her.

His fingers came to her chin and tipped her head up. "I wouldn't want any gentleman out there getting ideas that you were available."

She tore her chin away as tears stung the back of her eyes. That flickering hopeful sensation was doused so thoroughly it left her cold.

"What's wrong?" his voice held a taunt that she hated. "Worried your lover will know that you've been freshly bedded?"

She flinched at his tone, but he clearly misunderstood.

"That's it, isn't it? You're worried that your old flame will know that you're no longer the innocent virgin he was after."

"That's not—"

"But you're not that girl anymore, Evangeline. You're my wife."

"I know that."

His jaw worked, and the possessiveness and anger she saw in his eyes had her lips parting with shock.

His gaze raked over her, and she felt more naked now than she had when she'd been bare before him. His thumb touched her lower lip. "Every man out there wants to do what I just did to you," he said. "But I'm the only one who touches you. Do you understand, Evangeline?"

She wanted to be angry. She wished she could muster some outrage. She'd already made her vows. She'd reassured him time and again. But all she could manage was a nod as he let her go.

"Come," he said, holding out his arm. "Your mother will be wondering where we've gone off to."

She nodded, letting him lead her out into the hallway and back to the torturously crowded ballroom.

She'd been so miserable when they'd first arrived. So horrified by all the stares and the whispers, and then all the questions and the small talk, her face stiff from fake smiles.

But now...

Now she couldn't bring herself to care if people stared as they passed.

Her heart had sunk so low she could barely keep up the small smile that was expected of her.

"Shall we?" Raff asked as a waltz began.

She nodded stiffly and didn't resist when he pulled her into his arms. They were silent for most of the dance, and when he asked her questions, her answers were short and simple.

It was all she could manage because her heart was aching.

It made no sense. But sense didn't seem to play much of a part in this marriage.

What had she thought? That just because he wanted her body, something had changed?

He'd only ever wanted her body. He'd never tried to tell her otherwise.

She'd been a fool to think that physical intimacy might mean more. She was a fool for wanting more.

When the dance ended, she made some excuse about needing a moment in the retiring room.

Raff's eyes narrowed on her, but he did not object.

Albert found her when she was on her way back to the ballroom. There were others about, there was nothing inappropriate about stopping to talk to an old friend.

And yet her gaze kept searching out Raff in the crowd, terrified he might see her talking to her former suitor.

"You are as beautiful as ever," Albert said, his voice low and intimate.

She stiffened. Where once that voice was so welcome, right now it made her ill at ease. Guilt rose up in her even though she'd done nothing wrong. "You shouldn't say such things."

When she met his gaze, she was horrified to see pity there. His eyes were soft with kindness, but sympathy, too.

She looked away quickly.

"Is he horrible to you, Angie?"

"Don't call me that," she said. But there was no heat in her voice.

Albert glanced around quickly and then leaned in. "I saw the way he spoke to you." His gaze dropped to her arm. "The way he handled you."

She swallowed hard, tears choking her throat and stinging her eyes.

"You deserve better, Angie," he continued.

She took a step away, her eyes filled with tears to the point that she was nearly blind. "We shouldn't be talking like this."

"Remember what I promised," he continued. "I will still rescue you. We can be together."

Rescue her. She stared at him through tear-filled eyes. He didn't honestly think she would run off with him, did he?

Yes, the promise had been noble and maybe even tempting on the day of her wedding when she'd been scared to death of the life before her.

But she'd said her vows.

She'd made her decision.

There was no way she could hurt her parents like that, nor Raff.

The thought of Raff had her clapping a hand over her mouth to stifle a sigh.

Oh drat. What on earth had she done?

"Angie?" His hand on her arm brought her back to the moment with a jolt.

"I should go," she whispered. "He'll be looking for me."

She hurried off to find Raff. He would be looking for her. Not because he cared but because she was his possession. That was all she was to him.

It was all she'd ever be.

That was enough for him…but for her?

She ran away from Albert, but she couldn't run from the truth.

For her, that would never be enough.

"MORE TEA, DEAR?" her mother asked.

She was avoiding her husband. The next day as she joined her mother for tea, she couldn't lie to herself about what she was doing.

All day she'd come up with reasons to be out of the house. To be anywhere but where he might be.

Now here, in her childhood home, she couldn't avoid the truth.

"You cannot stay here forever, you know," her mother said.

Evangeline sighed. No. She couldn't. This wasn't her home any longer, and to come here out of some childish urge to run away…

It wasn't fair. Not to Raff and not to her parents.

"I know. I'll return home in time for dinner."

"Good girl," her mother said.

Silence fell. To be fair, silence was not unusual between her and her mother. But right now, it felt heavy. It was a reminder that she wasn't wanted here either.

She'd never truly fit here—she wasn't the daughter they'd wanted her to be. But she'd done her job. She'd married well. That was all they'd wanted for her and from her.

She took a sip of tea and sighed.

She'd done her duty. She supposed there was some pride to be had in that.

After her run-in with Albert the night before, she could even admit that perhaps her parents had been right not to indulge her first infatuation.

They must have known that as the first man to show her any attention and to be so kind to her, her feelings were indeed childish. She could see it now so very clearly.

And her feelings for Raff?

Were they merely the result of his attention? Or were they born of some fantasy of the sort of marriage she'd hoped for?

Was there any truth to these feelings, or was she just creating fairytales out of thin air?

She and her mother might not have been close, but she didn't know who else to ask about these matters. And she desperately needed some insight.

Was it normal to develop an infatuation with one's husband? And what was one to do if those feelings were not returned?

She set her teacup down with a loud *clink* that seemed to startle her mother.

"Mother, there is something I should like to discuss." She bit her lip. "It's about my husband."

She cleared her throat and drew in a deep breath, but her mother cut her off with a loud exhale.

"I knew this day would come," she said, her chin rising stoically as she folded her hands in her lap. "And I am sorry."

Evangeline blinked. "Pardon."

"Your father, too," her mother said. By the way she spoke through a clenched jaw, it seemed as though Evangeline were prying the words out of her.

"You're...sorry?" she asked, confusion temporarily replacing all her other worries.

"I knew he would tell you," her mother continued. Her voice held a tinge of bitterness, and her fingers worried the hem of her gloves, her gaze everywhere but on Evangeline. "And really, we ought to have told you months ago."

Evangeline's jaw hung slack as she tried to keep up with this turn in the conversation.

"As I'm sure your husband told you, your father's losses were great." Her mother kept her gaze on her skirts as she fussed with a seam. "Mr. Foley, obviously, could not marry you without a dowry. He made that clear, and I'm sure he explained as much himself on your wedding day."

"My dowry?" Evangeline echoed the one word that made sense.

She had no dowry?

Albert had said he could not marry her?

Her mother winced. "It must have been a terrible shock. I'm

sorry your father and I did not prepare you properly. But, as you know, His Grace can be terribly persuasive, and when he not only offered to marry you without a dowry but to pay off your father's debts, as well, you can imagine how relieved we were."

Her mother kept talking, but Evangeline could hardly hear a word.

Betrayal made her feel sick, but she managed to nod and murmur what she hoped were appropriate words of understanding.

All this time, she'd thought she'd had some semblance of freedom. She'd thought her wishes might be taken into consideration, but that had never been the case.

She'd been a pawn.

Raff hadn't stolen her. She'd been sold to pay off a debt.

"Who did you expect me to marry if not Mr. Foley?" she asked, pleased by how calm she sounded despite the roiling in her belly.

"Well, your father's friends were quite keen to make your acquaintance," her mother said.

Horror had Evangeline's stomach turning. She vividly recalled those friends. The old, portly men, with the lascivious smiles and the foul breath who'd swarmed around her like flies at the ball.

"I know you had an affection for Mr. Foley, but we felt certain that once he explained that there could be no marriage, you would come around to finding one of your father's acquaintances...acceptable."

She swallowed hard. Her mother seemed to think that Albert had explained that he could not marry her.

Her brows came down.

But she dismissed those thoughts because Albert was not nearly as important as her husband.

"Of course," her mother continued, forced amusement in her tone. "We could not have foreseen that the duke would be so smitten. How very fortunate for us all."

"How very fortunate," she murmured in agreement.

How very fortunate that Raff had come along and paid off her father's debts.

Her stomach pitched and roiled dangerously as memories came back to her.

How he must have laughed on their wedding night when she'd accused him of wanting her dowry. She'd been so sure that he'd wronged her, but…

He hadn't.

Tears stung the back of her eyes as her mother continued with her explanations and rationalizations.

Raff hadn't told her the truth about her parents either.

Why? To spare her feelings or out of pity? She wriggled in her seat as unease and fear and anger all warred for supremacy inside her.

She wasn't sure if she should be angry with Raff or grateful.

Mostly she was angry, though. With him for keeping her in the dark. With her parents for selling her off without a care to her wishes. With Albert for not being open and honest about his situation…and hers.

Coming to her feet, Evangeline felt a new surge of power. She wasn't innocent any longer. She was a duchess. She was a wife.

Maybe one day soon, she'd even be a mother.

"Thank you for the tea," she said to her mother with a forced smile.

For all his faults, Raff had given her a better life than the one her parents had planned. And much as it stung her pride and hurt her heart, his willingness to give her a modicum of freedom was a gift.

But she didn't just want freedom. She wanted love. The sort of devotion and understanding that she'd never had before.

And she wanted that with Raff.

CHAPTER SEVENTEEN

R AFF EYED HIS guest with all the disdain he was feeling.
To say Mr. Foley's visit was unwelcome was an understatement. He hadn't seen his own wife in more than twenty-four hours, and yet here he was—hosting her lover.

He didn't try to hide his sneer as he faced the other man across his desk. "What was so urgent that you had the audacity to arrive unannounced?"

Mr. Foley smiled.

The smirk didn't reach his eyes, and Raff's gut twisted with dread. Not that he'd ever let the other man see it.

But there was something horribly knowing in Foley's gaze. Something cold.

Cruel, even.

"I had the pleasure of speaking with your lovely bride at the Bermans' ball the other night, Your Grace."

Raff's jaw was clenched so tight it was in danger of breaking a tooth, but there was no way he'd give Foley the satisfaction of seeing his discomfort.

The fact that he'd ever experienced a moment of jealousy over this lowly, weak-chinned, smug arse was bad enough. He wouldn't let him know it.

He made a show of casting a bored glance toward the clock on the mantel. "Was that all you came to tell me?" He turned to glare at Foley. "Because I should tell you, I have no patience for men who waste my time."

"Indeed, Your Grace." He lowered his head in a humble gesture, but that smirk grew. "I happened to notice that you were not fond of my speaking to Her Grace." His gaze darted up to meet Raff's, and Raff was reminded of a snake.

A slick, slimy, venomous snake.

"Get to your point, Foley, and make it quick."

Foley leaned back, dropping any pretense of humility. "I'm assuming by your display of possessiveness that you are aware of Her Grace's feelings for me."

Rage had Raff's blood boiling. But it was the stab of pain that caused him the most discomfort.

Because Foley was right. She did have feelings for him—for *him*, this maggot of a man whose artifice was so superficial as to be laughable.

But even so, she'd fallen for him.

While she merely tolerated Raff.

He tapped his fingers on the desk before him, letting the silence grow until Foley's smirk faded, and he shifted in his seat.

"Any feelings my wife might have had for you are inconsequential," he finally said, his voice cold and even as he glanced pointedly toward the door. "Now, if you'll excuse me…"

"I'll admit, Your Grace, that Evangeline is the dutiful sort." Foley's lips curled up in a smile—the snake was getting ready to strike. "Pretty, too, no one could doubt that."

"You will cease speaking of my wife now if you know what's good for you," Raff snapped. He instantly regretted the show of temper when Foley's smile grew even more smug.

"I thought I'd won quite the boon when my family took over the neighboring estate," Foley continued, folding his hands over his belly as he leaned back. The knave was making himself comfortable as if this was his domain.

Raff's lip curled up in a sneer as he thought of all the ways he might teach this buffoon a well-deserved lesson in humility.

"Oh, yes," Foley continued. "A sweet, innocent beauty like Evangeline? It was almost too easy to woo her." Foley sniffed. "A few kind words and the poor lonely girl was eating out of the palm of my hand—"

Raff's fist came down on the desk with a loud bang as he shot to his feet. "You will not speak of my wife in such a way," he growled.

Foley's smile grew as he held up his hands. His eyes were beady and so cold and smug it sent wariness slithering through him, cutting through his hot ire like a blade made of ice.

"It had all seemed too easy," Foley said with a shrug. "A pretty, young, biddable bride who could give me the dowry I so badly needed."

Money. Raff's disgust grew. Of course this was about money.

"Imagine my dismay when her father finally admitted the truth." He arched his brows in a knowing look. As if they were compatriots in some way. "I know you know what I mean. Her father was careless."

Foley's lips finally fell into a scowl at the memory. He threw his hands out wide. "All my plans…*poof*. Gone just like that."

"How upsetting for you," Raff said. A muscle ticked in his jaw, his insides twisted with disgust and rage on his wife's behalf. But he'd be damned if he let Foley see just how badly his words stung.

Foley chuckled. "It was, rather."

"Get out." Raff's voice was so cold and sharp that Foley jerked back in his seat before coming to stand.

"But you see, Your Grace, I haven't yet made my proposition."

"I don't want to hear any propositions from you," Raff said. "You might have had a friendship with my wife once, but she will have nothing to do with you from here on out. Is that understood?"

Foley's smile widened. "There, you see, is where I was hoping we might come to an agreeable arrangement."

"An agreeable—are you out of your mind, man?" he roared. His hopes of keeping his temper in check entirely gone.

He heard noises coming from the hallway. His staff, no doubt, ready to burst in if he needed assistance tossing this man out on his ear.

As if he'd need help with this little weasel.

"You see, Your Grace," Foley continued mildly, his smile still in place, his eyes still cold as ice. "I was disappointed when I discovered that what I thought was a boon, was in fact, a counterfeit. A fraud that—"

"Did you just call my wife a fraud?" he growled, his fists clenching against his desk.

"Not her, per se, just the situation," Foley said easily. "But then you came along, Your Grace." Foley smiled like they were old friends.

"Yes, I spared her from a life with a wretch the likes of you."

"Well, you *tried*," Foley said, his voice so soft and innocent it made Raff's stomach turn.

Raff narrowed his eyes. "What's that supposed to mean?"

Foley held his hands out again, this time in an innocent, helpless gesture. "Your Grace," he said in a smooth, silky voice. "I saw Evangeline the other night. I spoke to her, and I saw how unhappy she is with you."

Raff's heart slammed against his ribcage, his pulse roaring in his ears. The earth was swept out from under his feet, and he held onto the edge of the desk.

This man didn't know what he was talking about.

He was a manipulative, greedy coward.

But try as he might to tell himself that, all Raff could think of was the way he'd taken her against a bloody door. How she hated outings like the Bermans' ball but had been so eager to attend...

Because Foley was there?

Had she been hoping to see him?

Jealousy rippled through him like venom, and he felt it tightening his limbs and roiling in his gut.

"She still wants me, Your Grace. She told me as much." The cad held his hands out with another helpless grimace, seemingly unaware that Raff's grip on sanity was frighteningly tenuous.

"Now, I, of course, respect the bonds of marriage." The slow intonation made it clear a *but* was coming.

Raff growled.

"But if your wife would prefer to run off with me..." He shrugged.

Raff didn't think. He came around the desk and punched the other man as hard as he could, sending him to the floor. "Just what do you think you're about?"

Foley groaned, rubbing at his jaw, but there was a glimmer of triumph in his eyes. "I told her on your wedding day that I would come for her if she were unhappy."

Raff stilled. For all this man's repulsive smugness, he didn't think Foley was lying.

"She would go with me," Foley said. So simply. So sure of himself.

Raff wanted to deny it. He wanted to say she'd never do such a thing.

But if she were in love? If he'd driven her away with his possessiveness and his high-handed ways?

She wouldn't. He couldn't quite bring himself to say it because he wasn't sure he'd sound convincing. Instead, he glared down as Foley scrambled to his feet.

"I'd hate to do it, honestly," Foley said like they were discussing a trip to the solicitor's office and not running off with Raff's wife. "But I will if I must."

"If you must?" Raff sneered in disbelief.

"We younger sons get nothing, you know," Foley said, his voice conversational.

The man was insane. He was standing here threatening a duke with not a hint of shame.

"If I want to get ahead, I need some leverage," he said.

Raff stalked toward him. "And you think my wife is a bargaining chip?"

Foley smiled, holding out his hands, palms up. "I don't have to take her away from you, Your Grace. That is precisely my point. I don't wish to make a fool of you, and truly, I'd be happy to let her rot in this prison of a marriage you've dragged her into. But it will cost you, I'm afraid."

This prison of a marriage.

The words were ridiculous…but were they true?

Had he trapped her with him, condemning her to a life she'd never wanted? Without the love she'd always wished for?

The love she deserved?

Guilt was an insidious beast, clawing at his insides, even as his rage at this man came to the forefront. Picking him up with a fist in his shirt, he tossed the man into the door. "You think you can threaten me?" he growled. "I am a duke. I can ruin your pathetic life."

"I mean no disrespect, Your Grace," Foley murmured from where he was once more sprawled out on the ground. His smirk belied his words. "But I can ruin yours, as well. Not even your reputation could withstand the scandal and humiliation of losing your wife to someone like me."

Raff stalked over to him, relishing the sight of the other man's tremble as he towered over him.

"You might be right, Foley," he said, his voice far calmer than he felt. "About all of it. But there is one very crucial way in which you are wrong."

Foley's brows drew together, his gaze flicking left and right as if he was thinking through every aspect of his plan. "What's that?"

"Evangeline might have been naive and sheltered when you first met her, but she is no fool. One moment in your company would be enough for my intelligent bride to see straight through you. And what's more…?" Raff lifted him off the ground and rammed his back against the doorframe, making him grunt in pain before Raff threw open the door and tossed him into the hallway. "I trust my wife."

Foley was silent for a second before he started to chuckle. But footmen were already appearing at the far end of the hall, and a moment later, they were dragging him away.

CHAPTER EIGHTEEN

EVANGELINE TREMBLED WHERE she stood leaning against the wall.

She heard Foley's parting shouts that he wasn't through here. She heard Raff slam the office door shut behind him.

She stayed where she was, shaking, her mind racing, as the house fell once more into silence.

I trust my wife.

She tilted her head back, trying to get her pulse under control.

She hadn't heard it all. But she'd heard enough. Betrayal had held her its frozen victim at first, and then…

Curiosity.

Shameful as it was, she'd been desperate to hear what Foley had planned. Even more desperate to know how Raff would react.

She'd come here to talk to him. To confront him on the fact that he'd never told her about her parents, but now…this.

Her head spun as she tried to make sense of it all, but her heart…

She clutched her chest as an ache made her gasp. Her heart knew very well what this meant.

He trusted her. And she…

She trusted him, as well.

Without knowing what she would say, her pounding heart drove her to his study door. She gave a short knock before letting herself in.

Her chest nearly split in two at the sight of him looking so ragged and overwrought. The cold, unfeeling, arrogant duke was nowhere to be found.

Maybe he'd never really existed at all.

That was just the mask he used to keep the world at bay. It was the defense he'd needed because, despite the servants and even his friends, Raff was alone in this world.

Just as alone as she'd been, if not more so, because he'd been expected to lead.

He stared at her in surprise for a long moment. "Evangeline, where did you…" He raked a hand through his hair. "That is, when did you return home?"

Home. The word wrapped around her and made her warm.

"Just now," she lied. She wasn't sure why. She just…

She didn't want him to have to explain. She didn't want him to worry about her or be upset for any reason.

She moved forward into the room, watching as he sank into his leather seat, exhaustion and so many other emotions there, but not for long.

He'd cover it up. He'd smile for her sake and make some high-handed pronouncement about their dinner plans.

A smile tugged at her lips. She didn't know much, but she knew her husband.

This house was new, their marriage still fraught with unchartered territory to explore. But this was her home.

He was her home.

With that thought, she moved in further, her heart galloping away from her as he frowned.

"You're flushed, Angel. Are you all right?"

She didn't stop until she was right in front of him. "Yes, I'm all right. I just want…"

I want you to know that I trust you, too.

I know you hid my parents' secrets from me, and I know why.

"I want you," she said simply.

His brows arched in surprise as she dropped to her knees before him. Nerves had her pulse clamoring, but she ignored the trembling in her fingers as she went to work unfastening his trousers.

His hand over hers made her still. "Angel," he said in a low, gruff voice. A voice filled with warning. "What are you doing?"

She peeked up at him, wetting her lips nervously. "Nothing you haven't done for me."

"Angel, I—" He stopped short with a groan when her hand slipped into his breeches and gripped his already hard member.

A teasing smile tugged at her lips. "What was that, Raff? I didn't hear you."

He let out a hiss of air as a wicked gleam filled his eyes, and a smile tugged at his lips. "Do you know what you're doing, Angel?"

She leaned in closer, settling herself between his thighs as she freed him, her eyes widening at the formidable sight. "No," she admitted. "But I was hoping you'd teach me."

His head fell back with a groan as his hands slid into her hair. "You're teasing the devil, love."

She pressed her lips to the tip of his erection and smiled against the hot, smooth flesh that throbbed insistently in her hands. "I don't see any devils here. Only my husband."

He groaned again. "Part your lips, love. That's it. Now slide my cock into that sweet mouth of yours." His breathing hitched as she did what he said, shocked when a now-familiar heavy sensation filled her low in her belly.

She moaned as he grew thicker in her mouth, the taste of him so perfectly male. So perfectly Raff.

Her breasts were straining against her corset, her thighs pressing together insistently to find relief.

He gripped her head, tugging her up. "I want to come inside you," he growled.

She didn't wait for him to guide her this time. She hitched up her skirts and straddled his lap with a desperate moan.

She surprised herself when she took him inside her, sliding down onto him, sheathing his length with her slick heat. He filled her in one hard thrust.

They both groaned at the feel of him so deep.

"Like this?" she whispered through labored breaths as she rocked her hips.

His hands gripped her thighs. "That's it, love," he panted. "Now touch yourself for me."

She didn't hesitate. She didn't even blush. She slipped her hand up beneath her skirts, rocking her hips desperately to get more of this unbearably sweet friction.

"Show me," he growled.

He pinched her nipples until she screamed and then dropped one hand to cup her buttocks and hold her still so he could grind up into her so deep she could hardly breathe.

"Come for me," he growled into her ear. That command was all it took to set her over the edge, shattering around him as she dug her nails into his shoulders and held on tight.

A few more violent thrusts, and he spilled his seed inside her, hot liquid filling her, claiming her.

She dropped her head against his shoulder and kissed his neck.

He might have claimed her with his body, but this time she'd claimed his, too. She wrapped her arms around him tight, letting out a squeak as he came to stand, holding her snug and safe in his arms as he strode toward the door.

"Where are we going?" she asked, a smile in her voice.

He turned his head to kiss her temple. "To our room."

"Our room?" She felt hopelessly girlish with the way her heart flipped and her voice broke.

She felt his smile. "My room is yours whenever you wish to join me there."

She threaded her fingers into his hair. "Then I would like to join you there tonight, please."

He clutched her so tight she could hardly breathe.

And she loved it.

When they were in his room, he set her down on the bed. "I want you again, Evangeline." His gaze roamed over her with a frown as if looking for injuries. "Is it too soon?"

She shook her head, already eager, a hunger starting anew as she watched him undress.

He paused with his back to her, and she was certain she could see his hesitation in the way his shoulders rose, the way he drew in a deep inhale.

"What is it?" she asked.

He cleared his throat, his head down, gaze fixed on his fingers as he slowly disrobed. "I don't want you to hear this from anyone else, Angel, so I'll tell it to you plain."

"All right," she said, her voice shaky even to her own ears.

She clutched her fingers into the covers, her toes curling as she braced herself to hear the awful truth.

That the man she'd thought she'd loved had only ever been lying to her. That he was threatening to destroy Raff unless he paid him off. That—

"Your former suitor is still in love with you."

She sat up. "I beg your pardon?"

"You'll hear it from the servants or some busybody soon enough, I'm sure." He gave her a wan smile, but his gaze didn't meet hers. "Mr. Foley has not taken his rejection lightly, I'm afraid."

She frowned.

He was lying. Why was he lying? He ought to be rubbing it in her face—if he were a cruel man, that's exactly what he would have done. But any man in his position would at the very least tell her what a fool she'd been. Tell her just how horrid Foley was.

"I had to run him out of the house," he continued. "He's besotted, the poor fool."

"Raff," she started warily.

"I know," he interrupted. "I know you've done nothing to encourage him, just as I know I have nothing to fear. As I told Mr. Foley." His gaze finally lifted to meet hers. "I trust you."

Her heart tripped and fell in her chest. I trust you. It wasn't flowery words of love. It wasn't even a mention of affection. But from this man…

She wet her lips. "I trust you, too," she whispered.

His gaze darkened. With desire, yes, but affection, too.

"Do you?" he asked. His voice was mild, but she knew how much that meant to him. He'd been on his own for so long, only letting in his friends from his school days. Only trusting those men who he thought of as family because he had no family of his own.

He was letting her in. That's what his words told her.

And the enormity of that left her throat choked.

"Thank you," she whispered.

His smile was crooked as he returned to the side of the bed, his gaze already greedy as it ran over her disheveled bodice.

"Thank you," he repeated, his tone lighter now with wry amusement. "For what? Trusting you to uphold your vows?"

She sat upright, her gaze holding his as she reached for him. "No," she said, her voice wavering with emotion. "For trying to spare me from the truth."

CHAPTER NINETEEN

Raff stilled, his gaze sharpening as her eyes welled with tears.

Bloody hell.

"Don't cry." It was a gruff command, far from gentle, and he felt like an absolute arse as she sniffed and tried to stifle it.

"I heard Foley," she said, her small hand fitting into his and giving it a tug until he sank beside her on the bed.

The scent of her, so sweet and heady, wrapped around him and made him want to banish Foley's name from existence so he could bury himself inside her again and forget every fear that knave had stirred inside him.

But instead, he faced her all-seeing gaze as every fear he'd ever harbored slid out from the depths where he'd tried to bury them.

Meanwhile, his mind was scrambling to adjust the lie. To spare her feelings. That was why he'd lied in the first place. He'd taken one look at those wide eyes, those sweet lips, the gentleness in her gaze, and he'd…he'd lied.

He'd do it again, too, if it meant banishing those tears from her eyes. He reached out to brush aside an errant tear, his voice still gruff but gentler now as he said, "Please don't cry, love. He's not worth it."

She sniffed and nodded. "I know that," she said. "I'm not

crying over him."

"How much…" He arched his brows. "That is, how much did you hear?"

"Enough," she said. "Enough to know that you lied about why he'd come." Her gaze was unrelenting.

Had he ever thought her biddable and simple? Lord, but he was a fool.

"Why did you lie?"

He winced, gesturing to her tears. "To avoid this."

He'd tried to add some levity to his tone, but her gaze was serious and even. "You lied to spare my feelings."

It wasn't a question, so he didn't reply.

She shifted, so she was coming up on her knees, putting her eyes nearly level with his. "And not telling me about my parents," she said, her hands on her hips. "Was that to spare my feelings, too?"

He flinched at the intensity of her stare.

"I'll take that as a yes," she said.

"How did you know?" he asked, curiosity winning out over self-preservation.

"I had tea with my mother today." Her gaze cut to his. "She seemed to think I already knew about the fact that I had no dowry, that Albert had washed his hands of me, and that I'd been destined to marry one of my father's lecherous old friends to pay off his debts."

Raff drew in an inhale with a hissing sound, his gaze moving over her face to try and suss out her emotions.

She couldn't be so calm about this. Not even the coldest woman would be unfeeling in the face of these revelations.

And his wife was anything but cold.

His heart ached when he caught the glimmer of hurt in her eyes that she was trying to hide.

Folding her into his arms, he held her tight, her heart pounding against his. "Ah, love," he murmured. "I'm sorry you learned of that."

"I'm not." Her voice was high with emotion but firm. Confident. "You were right," she said, pushing against his chest gently until she met his gaze. "When you told Foley that I'd been naive—"

"Sweetheart, I did not mean—"

"No, Raff." She pressed a finger to his lips gently, smiling sweetly when he caught the tip lightly between his teeth. "I'm telling you that you were right. I was hopelessly naive. In many ways, I still am. I grew up living in daydreams and fantasy worlds of my own creation."

He felt a surge of warmth and tenderness as her cheeks pinkened, and her smile turned shy.

"I know now that Foley was an extension of that. I didn't know him. Not truly. But he seemed a safe place to pour all my silly fantasies." She clutched his arms when he stiffened. "I never felt anything real toward him. He just seemed like freedom to me after a lifetime of disappointing my parents and feeling like an outsider in my own home."

He nodded. "I can understand that."

"Can you?"

She looked so hopeful, and that hope seemed to jar loose a truth of his own.

"I suppose I did something similar with you," he said. "I knew from the first moment that I wanted you. And your sweetness, your timidness, your innocence…" He let out a huff of exasperation as he tried to figure out how to say it without hurting her feelings. "I suppose I took one look at you and thought I could have it all without the risks."

Her brow furrowed. "How so?"

A pain he hadn't acknowledged for a decade crept into his voice. "I looked at you and saw what it might be to have a sweet, docile wife, who would admire and love me unconditionally. Who would give me the family I'd always craved without expecting anything in return."

She bit her lip, amusement glinting in her eyes. "And instead, you got me."

A surprised laugh escaped him, and he cupped her cheeks in his hands with a tender kiss. "Luckily for me, yes. I know now that what I'd thought I'd wanted wouldn't have been enough. I hadn't wanted to admit to myself that I wanted more. I wanted real. I wanted...." He swallowed, his gaze colliding with hers. "I want you, Evangeline. Not just in name and not only your body." He leaned in, his chest threatening to burst as his heart swelled dangerously. "I want all of you."

She leaned into him until her lips grazed his. "You have me," she whispered against his lips. "All of me."

He couldn't speak as emotions choked him.

She ran her fingers through his hair. "That's what I've been trying to say, Raff. I might not have picked you for myself, but I am grateful all the same."

After a tense moment, he brought himself to ask the question that had plagued him ever since Foley's departure. "And you don't think...that is, I am not..." He cleared his throat. "I've not forced you into some new prison?"

She shook her head quickly, her eyes brimming with tears. "No, Raff. No. And I hate Foley for even suggesting as much."

"I know I am not the warmest of men. I don't know how to be a husband—"

"And I don't know how to be a wife. But you are kind, Raff. I knew that before today. I knew that almost from the start, truthfully."

"You did?"

She smiled, and it felt as though the clouds parted with that sweet, angelic smile. "I know you meant to torture me by making me beg, but by not forcing me to be intimate, you gave me a gift. And then you gave me more gifts each and every time you taught me what pleasure meant."

Her arms wrapped around his waist as she spoke, and she pressed her soft curves into his hard planes. He held her tight, sliding one hand down to cup her bottom and drag her closer, so his hard length was nestled between her thighs.

She gasped, her eyelids fluttering as her lips parted.

"Mmm, you know you taught me a valuable lesson in turn, don't you?" he asked as he nibbled at her lower lip.

"I did?"

"You did. Up until you, I'd never understood how meaningful sex could be. I'd thought it solely physical. A release. A quick pleasure. But you…" He closed his lips over her neck and grinned at her low moan. "You made it feel like so much more than two bodies coming together."

Her soft giggle had him pulling back in surprise.

"Perhaps I'll make a romantic of you yet," she teased.

He chuckled before kissing her hard, slanting his mouth over hers to taste every bit of her. "You could try," he taunted. "And in return, I'll teach my angel the joys of the flesh."

"Raff." She pulled back, her eyes wide and urgent.

"What is it?"

"I want it all with you. I may still be naive, and perhaps even childish, but I want to learn, and I want to have experiences, and I want…I want everything."

His heart was a mangled wreck at the earnest affection in her eyes.

"What's everything, love? Because I'd give you the world if that's what you asked for."

Her smile trembled, and he caught the flare of vulnerability.

She slid her hand down, stroking him through his breeches. "I want a family…with you."

He groaned, his hips jerking as he pressed himself into her hand.

He leaned forward, tipping her over, so he could lie on top of her, already pulling off her dress, so he could lavish her lush breasts with open-mouthed kisses. "I want to fill you with my seed and have you round with my child," he agreed.

She cupped his face, dragging him up so their eyes met.

"I want you to be there with me. I don't want to be apart."

She looked so scared, as if he might ever refuse such an offer.

His chest tightened painfully as he gazed down at her. "You want a home with me, love?"

She nodded quickly, biting her lip. "I know you said you wanted your freedom but—"

He kissed her hard to silence her. "I was a fool. I thought happiness meant being able to do as I pleased with whomever I pleased. But what I want—what I've always wanted is a—home." He swallowed hard as his hands trailed over her perfect features. "A family."

She nodded, her eyes wet with tears. "Me, too."

He leaned down until his nose grazed hers. "I want love."

He felt her smile against his lips. He tasted her tears. "I want love, too."

"Then you shall have it," he whispered, his voice harsh with emotion as he lifted her skirts.

Her hands scrambled to help, and soon, they were naked in their need to seal this new vow.

She was wet and hot and whimpering with need by the time he had her naked beneath him. She spread her legs wide in welcome, a seductive smile tugging at her lips as she ran her fingers down teasingly, stroking herself as she gazed up at him from beneath heavy lids.

"Show me how much you love me, Raff," she whispered.

He fell over her, thrusting his cock all the way into her tight channel in one hard thrust. "Every day, my love. I'll show you every day."

Her head fell back as she lifted her hips to meet his, their bodies moving in harmony as they held each other close. He showered her with kisses as she stroked him and held him close.

All the while, they murmured their vows—promises of loyalty, of trust, of a future.

Promises of undying love.

EPILOGUE

One year later...

EVANGELINE HAD NEVER seen her husband so cross.

"No, Angel, I mean it." He glowered at her from where he stood in front of the fireplace in their bedroom.

They rarely left the country these days, except to visit with friends, and with the fire crackling and her husband looking so devilishly handsome in its glow, Evangeline felt a swell of such utter contentment, it brought tears to her eyes.

"Oh, darling, please don't cry." Raff's gaze grew soft and tender as he moved toward her and took her into his arms.

"I cannot help it," she said with a sniff.

And she truly couldn't. Ever since her belly had started to grow round with their child, she'd lost all control of her emotions. Her lower lip trembled now as she gazed up at her doting husband. "Are you not attracted to me any longer, is that it?"

Her husband's growl said he was unamused by her teasing, and she choked on a laugh.

If anything, Raff had become even more desirous of her body ever since she'd gotten with child.

She caught him watching her constantly with that dark, hooded gaze.

A gaze that never failed to make her ache.

A gaze that had ascertained she was carrying an heir within months of their wedding day.

Oh, yes, her husband had only grown more insatiable, it seemed. But also, ever more protective with each passing second.

She gazed up at him now as she let her hands trail up over his chest. "Please, my love," she said.

He gave a grunt. Meant to be a no, she supposed, but if he was losing the battle with words, then she knew she'd win in the end.

She pressed against him harder, letting him feel her swollen breasts that he'd been eyeing all day on their journey back from visiting the Earl of Foster.

Newly married himself, the visit had been filled with laughter and love. The earl's wife was quickly becoming one of Evangeline's dear friends, and seeing Raff's close friend so very changed by love had made her weep more than once, much to everyone's amusement.

Each time, Raff had pulled her close and kissed away her tears, whispering words of love for her and their unborn child.

His gaze dipped down to her bosom, visible through the lacy negligee he'd had made for her. "Angel, you're tempting the devil, and you know it."

His hands gripped her bottom and tugged her closer until they both moaned at the feel of his pulsing cock nestled between her thighs.

"Not a devil," she teased. "My husband."

She went up on tiptoes to kiss him, and his mouth met hers with hunger.

When they were both panting for breath, the flames of desire stoked to unbearable heights, she took him by the hand as she backed up toward the bed. "This is me," she said in a low, husky voice filled with need. "This is me begging."

He groaned, his expression pained as he let her lead him to the bed. "My love, you know I will bring you pleasure—"

"No." She stopped short with a scowl. If he thought he was

the only one who could be stubborn and glower like a devil, he was very much mistaken. "I want you inside of me."

He groaned again, his eyes dazed with passion as he took her in from head to toe.

"To speak plainly, my love," she said as she sank onto the bed and lay back against the pillows. "I want you buried inside of me. And I won't settle for anything less."

He looked beside himself with desire, his pupils dilated and his breathing harsh. "You know I want that, Angel."

She went up on her elbows with a pout. He'd been pleasuring her nonstop since they'd been married, but of late, he'd used only his fingers and his mouth. He'd been holding back with his member, and she was growing tired of his hesitation.

"Why won't you bed me?"

Climbing up onto the bed beside her, he palmed her sensitive breasts until she was moaning and writhing. Begging.

She was back to begging as she reached for the flap of his breeches.

"Angel, no," he started to protest. "You are in a delicate condition. What if I hurt you?" He pulled back with a wince. "What if I harm our child?"

"You won't," she said gently, her annoyance fading fast because she knew precisely what this was about.

It had little to do with his fears of physically harming her and the child. She reached up a hand to stroke his cheek: her precious, loving, surprisingly sensitive duke.

Even Benedict had noticed, and he'd taken her aside to explain, though all he said confirmed what she'd suspected.

He wants a family.

Benedict's wife had looked on with obvious affection as the earl had spoken to her *You have been the answer to his prayers, Evangeline. But I think...that is, Hayden, Malcolm, and I have come to believe that he's gone so long on his own, he doesn't know how to be a family man.*

She nodded. She'd been watching her husband grow more

and more overprotective, more and more fearful as their marriage grew happier and happier.

"Love," she said slowly. "I don't know how to be a mother either. This is new for both of us."

"Yes, but at least you've had one," he said, his gaze open and so filled with uncertainty, her heart turned over in her chest. "I barely remember my father, and those memories I have are not pleasant. I don't want to hurt you," he said. "I don't want to hurt our child."

She went up on her elbows so she could kiss him. "You couldn't hurt us, Raff. Not with all the love you have in your heart."

He kissed her hard, pressing her back into the pillows until he was hovering over her. His gaze raked over her face. "Are you certain about that?"

She took one of his hands and pressed his palm to her heart. "You claimed this a long time ago," she said. "And you've never given me reason to doubt that it is in the very best hands."

"I want to make you happy—"

"And I am." She reached up with her free hand to touch his cheek. "You gave me a home. You gave me understanding and appreciation and love. No one in the world could make me happier than you do."

His eyes glinted in the dark. "Do you know how much I love you, Angel?"

She swallowed down a sob as emotions tightened her chest and left her breathless. "Not half so much as I love you."

He grinned as he kissed her sweetly. "Is that a challenge?"

She laughed. "A bet."

"Mmm." He kissed her neck as he fondled one of her breasts, making them both moan. "I do love gambling with you, love. The boons are so very delicious."

She arched her back for more, a fire burning in her belly. "Take me, husband," she ordered with a gasp. "Take me now. Don't make me beg again."

His chuckle was low and more devilish than ever. "If you're certain, my love." At long last, he fitted his hard staff against her entrance. And as he slid inside of her, he lowered his lips to her ear. "I love you, Angel. And I love our child. Marrying you was the best thing to ever happen to me."

She opened her mouth to tell him she felt exactly the same but cried out in ecstasy instead. At last, her husband was inside of her.

Precisely where he ought to be.

Join Bella Moxie's newsletter to find out what happened between Malcolm and his runaway bride with the free novella, *The Fallen Earl's Sinful Temptation:* **eepurl.com/gW_QWL**

About the Author

Bella Moxie is the author of the steamy regency romance series, *Dukes Gone Dirty*, as well as the offshoot novella series, *Rogues Gone Dirty*. Her books are spicy, but filled with sweet, satisfying, over-the-top love that not even the most alpha hero can resist.

Grab a free, steamy regency romance novella when you join Bella's newsletter at:
eepurl.com/gW_QWL